THE BOOK OFJOEL

ANDREW SWEET

JOEL EMERSON HAINES searched for God in the brown haired woman prostrating herself before his mother. Even the soft glow of the crucifix hanging over the woman's wrenched body stirred nothing in his heart; he despaired. He may as well not have existed for their sense of his presence in the room. The woman wailed. It was similar to a scream, but Joel thought it different in that a wail was a full body event. Screams could emanate from something as trivial as dropping a communicator on a toe, but a wail — that was special. Nothing drove home the message of repentance like a good wail, or so his mother told him.

And that's what this woman did. The woman and his mother were nearly the same age if he had to guess — in their mid-thirties, or twenty-nine as went the white lie that his mother said wouldn't send her to Hell. Sweat trickled down his back between his shoulder blades as he played witness to the scene before him. The woman's wails cut through the air and pierced his ears, working their way into his nerves.

He knew better than to interrupt.

"Get up, Caitlyn, the Lord sees you."

The way Evie Haines, Joel's mother, smiled down at parishioners, especially wailing ones, made her seem like Mother Theresa crossed with the Mona Lisa. The thick black hair was pulled up into a tight bun because she was always presentable. Her dark walnut colored skin and ebony irises set into those big white eyes expressed so much warmth and compassion that Joel almost believed there could be some left over for him.

Caitlyn, shorter than his mother by an inch and with hair that was so white it shimmered blue, pushed herself to her knees while his mother hooked an arm underneath one of the woman's arms. A quick glance told Joel that he needed to get up and help, and that he wasn't as invisible as he thought. Without hesitating Joel rushed over the thick carpet to support the woman's other arm and the two lifted her into a nearby chair.

"I don't know what to do, Evie. I've been giving to the Lord. I come to church. I even come to Bible study every week. Why would He do this to me?"

"The Lord has a place for you, Caitlyn. There's a meaning here, you just have to trust."

"The cancer is back. I pray and pray, but it doesn't make a difference. The doctor says it's metastasizing, and the only treatment is the nanites. What does the Lord even think about those disgusting little creatures flowing through my blood, eating pieces of my body?"

Joel let go of the woman's arm and stepped back behind her, trying his best to blend into the wall in that cramped office.

"Caitlyn, what do I always say?"

"Keep giving, and the Lord will provide?"

"Exactly. Get the treatment or don't get it. The Lord works how the Lord will. But the Lord needs what's his."

"The treatment — it's one hundred and forty thousand dollars. That's all of our savings, Evie. I mean, it'll be one or the other, I'm sure."

"The Lord takes care of his own, Caitlyn. If you just make sure the Lord gets his share, then he'll do what's right."

Every weekend, Joel personally witnessed over two-thousand people give the Lord his share in the form of checks, or cash, though more usually cash-coins of varying denominations. The digital currency was like a bearer bond, and tracked how much was left on it at any given time. The largest denomination he'd ever cashed in for the church was twenty-thousand on one coin.

"Well, Caitlyn, I can't tell you what to do. Only the Lord can. But I can tell you what I would do. I would make sure the Lord got his share and I would trust the Lord to look after me. Just ask in your heart, Caitlyn. Ask your heart what the Lord would want."

The woman closed her eyes and raised her hands, feeling out for something Joel had never felt — the touch of the Lord. One second. Then two. Then she lowered her hands to her arm rests. She blew out a thin breath.

"You're right, of course, Evie. You're always right. This is a test of faith. That's what it is. The Lord is testing me."

Joel's stomach churned with an unfamiliar feeling, and he felt sweat collecting on his palms as his hands clenched into fists. One thing he knew not to do was correct his mother. That was in the Bible — obey your parents.

"What happens if I die, though, Evie? You know how Ethan feels about how much I give. He'll stop, you know he will."

His mother looked at the woman with eyes furrowed in deep concern.

"I thought you'd willed it all to the Church? And the Lord loves you for it."

"He said he'll fight it. He said I need to get the treatment, or he'll put you in court for years to come."

He saw the glint of anger that his mother then managed to hide in less than a millisecond.

"Caitlyn, the Lord getting his helps Ethan, whether he wants to admit it or not. The Lord is looking out for you and yours."

"I know. What can I do though?"

"Why wait? Bring the money on Sunday, and once the Lord has it, Ethan can do whatever he likes. And we'll all pray for you. A thousand people, Caitlyn, all asking the Lord for your recovery."

The woman nodded, bobbing her head up and down on a neck that seemed too thin to support it.

"Good, Caitlyn. The Lord provides. Bring the money and the Lord will do as the Lord wills. Bless you, child." With another glance, his mother sent the clear message that it was time for Caitlyn to leave. Joel swooped in to grab the woman's arm and lift her to her feet before escorting her through the door, closing it behind her. He turned to his mother, whose eyes beamed. A smile stretched across to her face.

"Joel, did you see the devotion in that woman? The Lord will be so pleased. I can feel His presence in the room right now."

Joel felt only indigestion and embarrassment, but forced a grin that he didn't feel, and nodded to confirm a presence that he couldn't sense. Two lies in the matter of a minute.

The list of reasons Joel would eventually wind up in Hell just kept growing.

______

When Saturday came, Joel's feelings about the incident hadn't improved. His ineffectual morning prayers didn't fill the emptiness that consumed him. Joel arose from his knees to tend to the multitude of events that brought the church to life.

The church building seemed huge when it was empty. Joel looked out over the pews where he knew screaming worshippers would congregate in just a few hours. The seats fanned out away from the stage at a slight incline, just enough so that people could see without having to stand — though most members chose to rise to their feet during the lengthy sermons. Terraced steps led up to the stage, with walkways bifurcating on either side to disappear into the preparation areas on the left and right. Behind the stage and elevated was a holographic projector. This he flicked on from his control panel in the back to project a replica of the lectern where his mother stood. With a dial and a few entries in a keypad, he brought up the statistics from the previous Sunday.

In addition to the hundreds who filled the auditorium each weekend, almost a million people signed into the virtual projection of it. Up from the week before by almost ten percent. He flicked the stats and holograph back off and then moved to test the audio.

"Joel?"

Joel glanced up to see his mother approaching him, already wearing a crisp navy kurta suit with gold embroidering along her cuffs and the inner lining of her sash. Her eyebrows were furrowed up into arches of concern as she slowed just three feet away from him, locked in.

"Test, one, two, three," he said, doing his best to ignore her for the moment. The speakers boomed his voice across the room causing her to jump. Joel bit his lip to keep from laughing. He knew better than to let a laugh escape in his mother's presence.

"Are you almost done setting up? There are people outside." Her arms folded across and one knee jutted out beneath the shawl, covered in pants that matched down to the gold cuffs.

"What time is it?"

There were no clocks in the main room because the Lord didn't like distractions. He considered mentioning this, and decided it was safer not to. She checked her watch and clipped out a response.

"Eight o'clock already. It's time to open."

"This is the last bit, Mom. I'm just finishing up."

He didn't look up at her directly, afraid that she would see the absence of God in his eyes. In the periphery is where he saw her impatient stance shift once, twice, then three times. He rubbed his hand over the back of his neck, trying to remember what needed to be plugged in where even under her intense scrutiny.

"What's the matter, baby?" He momentarily forgot that her question wasn't of concern — not for him anyway. He spun his head around, and she folded her eyebrows into a glare. In her defense, she did try on a smile, but it was lost in the brutality of her stare. He decided he had nothing of which to complain, and only shook his head before turning back to his work.

"If there is, you know you can talk to me, right? I'm your mother before anything else."

Words. Joel fought the temptation to accept her invitation, however genuine she made the offer sound. No sooner would he talk than everything he said would be locked into the vault of her mind, only to be brought out when it suited her as ammunition.

"I'm okay, Mom."

Another lie. Add that one to the list.

"I'm just asking." She paused for a moment and turned to face the doors again, a movement he saw from the corner of his eyes. Then she marched off toward her ready room.

He looked without moving his head to see in the same direction that had caught her attention. He saw the bodies then, pressed against the translucent windows like zombies in the holovids his mother didn't know he watched. She marched off with crisp steps back toward the ready room, where he knew she would spend the next ten minutes either praying or drinking coffee and reading up on the information they'd collected about the parishioners. Probably Caitlyn would be among those she read up on.

Finishing the sound check five minutes later, he made his way from the stage just as the loud metallic clank announced the opening of the doors. His mother had always been impatient, and people flooded in quickly like ants filing toward an abandoned cookie. Joel watched for a minute, mesmerized by how they just kept coming, and then by the thought of how ten times more watched her virtually.

Even in her weakened state, Caitlyn had managed to push to the front and took her seat just before the stage. As soon as the pews behind her filled, Joel flipped the switch to start the opening music so that the people wouldn't need to sit for long in boredom. That was also the signal to his mother to come out and start. Right on cue, she emerged from the ready room to a booming applause, all smiles and raised hands.

"Welcome, welcome friends," she began as the music and applause died down. "We're here today to learn and further the cause of the Lord. Does anybody remember what we talked about last week?"

Almost a hundred hands shot into the air, and Joel reached for his microphone. When she pointed, he darted from his sound booth down into the crowd to deliver the microphone to a skinny man with dark, bushy eyebrows.

"We talked about Satan, and we talked about *shills* — and how those *shills* were created in man's image."

Joel felt his teeth grind together as his jaw tightened. A sharp pain pierced through the joint where his upper and lower teeth hinged. The word set him on edge. *Shill* wasn't even allowed to be spoken in their house, just like *fuck* or any other *shinga* or a multitude of other bad words. But home wasn't church, and on the stage, his mother let her hatred of genetically-modified clones that were more acceptably referred to as 'models' shine out over the crowd.

"Good, Jim Kent, that's really good. You do remember. Do you recall how the Lord feels about that?"

"They are abominations unto the Lord. These are the sons and daughters of Ham, who witnessed his father naked, to be cursed for all time."

As the impact of the word fell, Joel tried to see that connection. But models were made in something like ceramic pods, and couldn't possibly be descendants from anyone in the Bible. As usual, it didn't matter what he though the knew about it. The idea resonated with the laypeople, and his mother kept pushing it, so he guessed that he was wrong about that just like his mother said he was wrong about everything else. He smiled at the man and reached for the microphone back, but the man didn't relinquish it at first. He had more to say.

"They are the unclean. They fill the brothels and bring sin to the good people, engineered for temptation. They work in the refuse and filth, as they should. They are incapable of any real emotion, as the name would suggest. They *model* people, like shadows of humans. Don't be tempted to believe that they are real."

That was partly true, though the man had strayed from the teachings of the day. Models did work in sex brothels and sewers and as custodians, jobs which most non-models now avoided.

Joel's mother interrupted to bring the point back. As she did, Joel reached again for the microphone and this time grabbed it away from the man before he could protest.

"Praise be to Jesus, Jim. Praise be. But the Lord gave them a place in His mercy, didn't he? He made them the laborers, the toilers, that they may work their way to His redemption. Amen."

The entire crowd echoed an eerie *Amen* in response, that lingered for a moment before she began again.

"Let's talk about that some more. Now, I *know* that some of you," she said as she scanned the crowd of people whose clothes merged to form a canvas of vivid teals, yellows, and blues from where Joel stood. "*Some* of you have been going to those rallies, haven't you? You've been coming in here, and listening to His word but not hearing it. You've been lying to us, and lying to the Lord."

She glared at first, horrible in Joel's vision, as she cut

through the crowd. A lady with purple hair in the front row visibly winced, a look that his mother homed in on instantly.

"Kelly Mandrake," she said, pointing to a woman wearing a bright pink sari, who tried to melt backwards into the row behind her but was blocked escape by her own seat. "Come up here please."

The woman's eyes went glassy and she shook her head. Anonymous hands pushed her forward and guided her in an irresistible wave toward the front. Joel had been in that wave before. Once it caught you up, there was no way out of it. She stopped at the edge of the terraced steps just below where his mother stood.

"Its okay, baby, come up to me. Confess to the Lord — the Lord forgives."

The woman took one shaky step up onto the first tier on her matching high-heels, then another, and finally, shoulders slumped in defeat, pushed her way up the rest. Tears streamed down her face.

"Kelly, the Lord loves you, but the Lord sees all, and He wants to know why you abandoned Him."

"I didn't abandon the Lord, I swear. Just... those poor people. Did you hear about the one who got crushed under a box of nails at the construction plant? His arm was smashed and useless, and they sent him to be destroyed. They killed him for it."

"That's their lot, Kelly. The Lord has made it so."

"I — I know, it's just so hard, Evie. I don't understand how the Lord can..."

"That's because you don't believe," his mother's words stung with accusation. "You don't have the faith that it takes to be here, do you? Will you trust the Lord in His almighty judgment? Will you open yourself to Him, and believe what He tells you?"

The woman staggered backwards as though his mother had struck her with a knife.

"I *do* believe," she protested, but since she didn't have a microphone and the crowd had already begun to boo, Joel only barely made out her words. She mouthed them again while staring out with teary eyes over the crowd of her friends and relatives and one-time confidants.

"Repent!" Joel's mother held up her Bible-hand and Joel quickly flipped the lights to subtly shine up from beneath her, giving her an otherworldly glow. "Repent and be forgiven."

"I don't under..."

"Repent before the Lord!"

The woman looked up and then back out at the crowd, and then fell to her knees.

"I'm sorry, I'm sorry. I won't do it again. Lord, please forgive me."

His mother brought the Bible down again and the most genuine-looking smile that Joel had ever seen, born of his mother's mastery, replaced the hellfire and damnation on her face.

"You are forgiven dear."

The woman had been reduced to a sobbing heap on the floor, and the crowd began to applause. One man near the front leapt over the steps to assist the woman back to her seat.

"Let's pray for her soul."

The crowd joined together for a moment of silence while Joel's mother led them in prayer. Once complete, she turned her ferocious eyes toward Caitlyn.

"There's one more we need to pray for today."

That's when Joel noticed the man beside Caitlyn. As his mother rattled off about Caitlyn's disease, a story he already knew, the man next to Caitlyn focused all of his energy on the stage. At first, Joel thought it was him the man's gaze was locked to. Then he realized that his mother was just beyond him from the man's vantage point. The man stared unblinking at her, nodding along, transfixed by her words. In his heart, Joel felt jealousy growing, as he longed for the security of such a deep faith and devotion. There, amidst the crowd of believers, this man with reddish-brown hair, light blue eyes, and a scraggly beard, dressed in an uncomplicated t-shirt and jeans, held more faith than Joel. When Joel's mother got to the part about the recurrence of the cancer, the man's eyes filled with tears as though he channeled the woman's pain.

"But she has made the decision to give everything to the Lord, and to trust Him with her life. Over a hundred thousand dollars of her hard earned money, money that she struggled her entire life to build, has come to the church this morning."

Joel turned his attention back toward Caitlyn. A man on the other side of her bore a look of shock, with furrowed angry eyes stabbing at his mother. That one wasn't a regular, and Joel guessed he'd come precisely to prevent something like that from happening, but Caitlyn had managed anyway. The man turned and worked his way back through the crowd.

"Let's pray for her, everyone. Let's heal Caitlyn Parker."

The crowd began to chant the mantra of healing, taken from a spattering of scriptures. Joel chanted them under his breath by reflex. The red-headed man screamed the words, eyes bright with hope and joy.

CHAPTER 2

A WEEK HAD PASSED since Caitlyn's desperation and fear plagued Joel's troubled mind. Second to his mental image of her anguish lurked the memory of the strange man in the front row, so full of emotion that he'd barely been able to stay on his feet. The salve of time strained ineffectually against Joel's lasting discomfort.

He'd managed to avoid his mother's overly-perceptive gaze for most of the week, but the time would come when she saw through his veil. One day she would know what was in his heart. When she did, Joe was certain that she would kick him out of the church like she had their father.

"Joel, do you want to share?"

He brought his focus to the classroom circle before him, wondering how and when someone had decided that sitting in a circle with nowhere to hide was the best way to interpret the convolutions of the Bible. Joel felt the eyes of the group as proctor stared down from beneath his gold and red turban.

"I was only thinking of the chores I have to do later," Joel responded, while wedging one finger beneath the clerical collar chafing his neck to let some air in.

"Would Jesus want you to think about that or would he want you to listen and hear his word?"

How should I know, Joel thought.

"Sorry, Brother. I will be more attentive."

A whisper caught his attention from a boy seated to his left.

"Died. In her sleep."

"What does Jesus mean to you, Joel?" The circle leader asked apparently having decided to make an example of him. Joel knew the Bible as intimately as the tiny black mole on his left shoulder, and if he had to, he would use verse as a defensive weapon. But that was only if the guy wouldn't leave him alone.

"He's the way, and the truth, and the life."

"John 14:6. Very good. Yes, and when He said life, He didn't mean that you could get to the Lord by hanging out with your friends or spacing during class and not studying His word. He meant that He, and only He, was the way to heaven."

"Amen, Brother."

The whisperer to Joel's left joined in the Amen, and the circle leader moved on to another member. Joel's attention wandered as well, as he focused his listening back to the susuration, which continued in a rumble that ebbed and waned to his left.

"Ms. Parker? Dead?" The other boy replied.

"Just like that. Dead. Ask Greg, if you think I'm lying."

Joel's gaze shifted toward Greg Parker, a tall, gangly almost-man with glasses and a perpetual smile — except for today. Bloodshot eyes revealed tears ready to fall and his head tilted forward as though he examined the carpet for imperfections. Joel averted his eyes as the undertones continued.

"Lost everything. Couldn't even afford to bury her. All their money went into the church, for all the good it did them."

"Ms. Parker was a very devout woman, David. She believed in the church and spreading the word of God. The church was her way of giving back. Greg should be proud of her sacrifice." The circle-leader had caught the last sentence, and there was a fair chance Greg had too. Joel picked up movement out of the corner of his eye as Greg stirred but said nothing, his mouth in a tight line. Greg tilted his body forward until he nearly fell from his chair, yet stood in time to catch himself, all without looking up. With a quick turn, he took slow steps toward the back of the room, acknowledging no one.

"You two," the circle leader motioned to the two whisperers. "You stay after and help me clean today. Thank you for volunteering."

Joel wanted more information. Caitlyn hadn't seemed so sick that she would die within the week. She had seemed a little slowed by her disease, but had stood well enough in that front row. She had waved her arms around like everyone else.

When the circle-leader finally decided to move on, Joel tried for David's attention.

"Hey, David," he whispered under his breath, careful not to change position or talk too loudly.

"Shut up, you'll get me in trouble again." David replied to him.

"No, he's looking the other way. Did the cancer kill her?"

David seemed to think about the question for a few

seconds, or maybe he only weighed whether or not he thought he would get caught if he replied.

"Greg said it wasn't the cancer, but they didn't know what else it might have been."

Joel cleared his throat to ask another question before he was interrupted.

"Do you have more to share with the class, Joel?"

He hadn't paid enough attention and the circle leader had gotten back around to him without his noticing.

"I was just consoling David. He wasn't trying to disrupt earlier — just trying to get some closure on his friend's mother's death."

"As I said, there's nothing else to discuss about it. She died and she's with the Lord now."

"She better be for that kind of money." Joel heard someone behind the circle leader speak, but couldn't identify the source. When the circle leader twisted back to look, Joel made out a mass of dark auburn hair and thick eyebrows sheltering dark green eyes fixated on his.

"Delilah?"

"If they hadn't given all that money, she could have afforded treatment. Then we wouldn't have to be sad about her death."

"The cancer didn't kill her," Joel repeated, feeling his chest tighten. "They don't know what she died of."

"If it wasn't the cancer, then what was it, *Joel*?" She asked the question with an accusing tone, and Joel felt the tightness condense into a knife just between his ribs.

"I don't know. It could have been anything."

"Joel, Delilah, let's be civil." The circle leader interrupted. "We're all a little emotional right now to have lost one of our own. Let's take some deep breaths and see what Jesus would tell us about it."

"Amen," Delilah said, staring straight through Joel, who held her gaze as long as he could but eventually caved under the weight her stern unblinking eyes.

Caitlyn had died. Joel had known the time would come, but he hadn't expected it so soon.

CHAPTER 3

"WE HAVE AN AGING CONGREGATION," his mother replied when Joel asked about Caitlyn, oblivious to the fact that Caitlyn wasn't any older than she. "The youth are all doing virtual now. Older people die sometimes," she muttered through the practiced solemn-yet-joyful smile that she plastered on the instant they exited the car. A hush flowed through the crowd at the sight of her in her black dress and veil laced with obsidian pearls. There was no point in talking further, as she'd transitioned back into pastor mode. Joel dutifully shut his lips and donned a concerned-but-grateful smile of his own. He couldn't deny her point. A good third of the congregation exceeded the age of sixty and the church seemed to draw more than its share of people seeking healing for chronic illnesses. His mother nudged him toward the hearse.

"Help with the coffin, Joel. It's important to be seen doing things like that. You have to understand that it's not about the good you do, but about the good you're *seen* doing."

Joel followed her instruction, finding that the other five

of the pallbearers had expected him. They hoisted the coffin on three and began the slow trudge from the car to the expectant hole in the earth. The coffin slipped on his shoulder twice, and both times he corrected his posture and continued lugging the dead weight forward. Caitlyn rested inside, and he didn't want to think about her being there, so he embraced his wandering mind's ability to distract him from the present. The church, meaning his mother, had decided to pay for Caitlyn's funeral. The woman's final contribution to the Lord had dwarfed the funeral costs, so it really was the least they could do. He saw the Parkers clustered together at the edge of the grave, weeping as the pallbearers approached the hole in the earth that would swallow up their loved one.

Burying her was a kindness, he told himself, to help them in their time. The Lord needed their money more than they needed their mother, sister, and from the looks of some ancients who probably should have been in wheelchairs, child.

Then he thought that drones could do the mundane work of carrying the coffin to the grave. Some of the wealthier clients had done it before. The small clover-shaped devices latched onto the same handles he held and lifted in unison, then deposited bodies seamlessly and carefully into the final rest. Some coffins even levitated on their own. These thoughts told Joel that he had spent far too much time in graveyards lately. It was a dumb thought to have, as the church never paid for drones.

He shrugged the coffin from his shoulder down to his waist and dropped his elbow at the same time, bringing his corner of the box down a little faster than the rest of the pallbearers, earning him a reproachful look from one. In the piercing clank of metal on metal, the mechanism for lowering the coffin latched on and the box was free from his grasp.

It was a pauper's funeral. They'd had to march across the mud and over unmarked graves to get to the plot. Adornment for it consisted of a simple cross with her name engraved along with the date of her passing — April 3, 2201

"Caitlyn Parker was a good woman," his mother began, and he tuned out the rest. He'd heard the speech so many times he could recite it himself. His mother would ramble on about Caitlyn's loyalty and faith, and read a few verses from the Bible, probably something from second Corinthians. As he turned to find a place to stand, he saw the man who had swayed and stamped and cried at church the week before. The show of faith continued as the man's eyes overflowed with tears and he pulled at his shirt as though he might tear it free. Out of the corner of Joel's eye, he caught a rebuking glance from his mother directed in the man's direction. The man stopped pulling at his clothes as soon as the look landed, though a mixture of tears and mucus dripped from the man's chin. Joel's mother continued without the slightest break in the monotonous tenor of her sermon voice.

Joel saw that he was the last pallbearer on the mound, so shuffled quickly, backing away from the grave. His back collided into someone, who to his failing luck, turned out to be Delilah. She shoved him sharply with her elbow, enough to let him know that she still disapproved of him.

"Leave me alone," he growled under his breath.

"They'll never be able to find this grave again after they leave. Look around," she retorted back to him as quietly as he'd addressed her. He did look, and rows and rows of similar white crosses poked up from the earth. In a few short years, the grave would be indistinguishable from the others. Even with a graveyard map and coordinate system, this one would be difficult to find.

"Your mother did that."

"Caitlyn lived with faith," he commented. He'd seen it. The spirit had flowed through Caitlyn the same way it did through his mother. There was always a bit of the Lord in the Haines home, and the Parkers had been the same.

"She died poor. You think Greg's going to Fouriedon University now?"

"There are more important things than school."

"Says the son of a preacher. You have no idea what the world is like."

He felt the eyes of his mother cut into him, and turned his face upwards toward her. She glared at him a moment, never pausing in her graveside speech, and he felt that sting that told him she knew what they talked about and he'd better find someone else to stand by. He shifted a bit to the left, but to his dismay, Delilah followed.

"I'm not attacking you, Joel. I like you — you seem nice. It's just unfair."

He shrugged. Delilah sometimes talked like this, but other times, she was as full of the spirit as anyone he'd ever seen. She oozed spirituality, especially compared to him. He gulped down a thick wad of saliva.

"It's not a crime to love the Lord," he said.

"It's not," she admitted. "I know that. I love the Lord too. I'm just saying..."

"Don't then," he said. "There's nothing else that needs to be said. I know what I believe, and I know what you believe. What else is there?"

"Does believing in the Lord really mean paying for

service instead of medical treatment, Joel? I only come because my mother's addicted to this crap."

"Worshiping the Lord isn't crap."

"You're hopeless. Never mind, go stand somewhere else."

He moved to get farther away, but to his surprise, she followed him again.

"Joel, there's no way that you can't see what I'm saying."

Joel stopped listening to her as well as his mother. Their words mingled together into white noise in his ears as he found his attention drawn to the same red-haired man who had cried at the church service before. The man pulled at his shirt and fell to his knees before dropping his head into his hands.

The white noise stopped.

Joel turned his attention back to his mother to see that she wiped away her own tears now. A whirring noise began as machines lowered the coffin deeper into the hole, before finally releasing it and winding thick straps back up from the abyss. Greg was the first to the edge, eyes still as red as they had been the week before. He scooped up a handful of muddy dirt and tossed it over. A sudden gust of wind blew apart the clump and hurled tiny pieces back out, turning part of Greg's dark black shirt a tannish-brown. Greg paused for a moment as his hand moved on its own to brush his shirt clean and then, as though it couldn't find the purpose of the act of moving, lowered back to his side. Greg stood there, staring over the grave, as the crowd looked on in silence. Whispers built up the longer he stood, lips pressed tight and eyes fixated on something in the distance. Finally, he made his way from the graveside and the crowd parted to let him leave.

It was only Greg and some extended family, Joel realized with a start. Greg's father wasn't there and his little sister wasn't there either. Greg's grandparents were there, and his uncle from out of state with two children in tow, but those were all. Delilah must have seen the same thing, because she elbowed him sharply again.

"See?"

The lonely almost-man walked away so slowly that Joel could swear that the sun crossed the sky faster, peeking out from behind swathes of clouds jumbled together. Then, a few minutes later, Greg was gone. Another gap emerged at the edge of Joel's periphery.

Some of Delilah's verbal punches must have landed. When Joel saw his mother's vehicle just beyond the tree-line, he felt his hands go clammy. The price tag on that could easily have covered five of the funerals they'd just experienced. He felt his mother's arm slide over his.

"I saw you talking to Delilah," she said. "She's a pretty girl. What did you talk about?"

His pulse quickened and he knew that she counted every second it took him to respond as he raced through topics that wouldn't offend.

"The weather, mostly."

"That's the worst lie you could have possibly chosen. What did you really talk about?"

Round two. Now it became more complicated since he had to come up with something offensive enough to seem true yet wouldn't earn him punishment. One topic met both criteria.

"Dad," he said, and his heart went cold.

"Oh."

"I don't understand why he left."

"There are those, like us, who *know* the Lord, Joel. We

practice His love every day. For some of us, though, we just don't understand how much the Lord has sacrificed for us."

"My father didn't believe?"

"He believed. He just didn't *believe* the same way we do. He wanted to find another way to the Lord, so he left us. You already know this, Joel. What was that girl telling you?"

Already she'd changed from Delilah to "that girl."

"*Delilah*," he said, emphasizing her name, "said that her mother missed Dad sometimes. They pray about him."

Add one more lie. This one at least was based in truth. He knew, as they all had known, that his father and Delilah's mother had been close friends since childhood. Further, she was so devout to the Lord that Joel could easily see her praying nightly since his father's departure.

"She would."

He looked at his mother in time to see her turning away, and became aware that the conversation was over. The bite in her voice stung even though it wasn't directed toward him.

The pair rode home in silence. Joel peered out through the one-way window into the darkness.

They went their separate ways upon arrival. His mother wet to pray, and Joel did his best to pray also. In the darkness of his room, he collapsed to the floor. The words of the Lord's prayer erupted form his mouth and he desperately pushed it out into the night, a personal message carrying with it the solemn goal of redemption.

"Forgive us our debts," he stuttered the phrase out into the world, the knife in his belly stabbing ever inward. Then he slipped to his side, staring and seeing nothing in the black.

"Are you out there? Lord?"

He waited, feeling out with his senses, looking for a response. The heat pressed in on him and sucked at his breath. Tremors of cold spiked through his veins as he lay there, each second of silence confirming his terror that he might never feel the Lord's grace. Still he lay holding his breath, reaching out into the dark with his mind, teasing meaning from every sound beyond his window. Each fell away as explanations emerged of their origins. He called out one last time, curled up alone in the night beneath a cross that took up his entire bedroom wall.

No answer returned, only the thick undulating static of cicadas chirping in the distance.

CHAPTER 4

JOEL STRETCHED in the early morning sun and fished through his clothes in preparation for Sunday's church ceremony. Grey slacks coupled with a light blue blazer and a thin cotton undershirt combined with dark tan shoes completed his look — every single item of clothing provided by his mother. The light colors helped in the Texas heat, though this late in the year he wouldn't feel that heat for another few hours.

The stresses of the previous day had evaporated and his rested mind didn't engage in the mental olympics from the day before. He knew the reprieve was temporary, as the early morning would eventually give way to the late morning which would give up itself to another church session and another painful Bible study. And more accusing looks from Delilah. But for now, he could escape his room and walk through the gardens in peace. If he was very lucky, the sun through the pecan trees could help ground him for the day and shore up his defenses against the onslaught of the faithful.

Other children had virtual reality to disappear into. Joel had played once, years before. Delilah had been his partner in crime then. She'd let him borrow her older brother's haptic suit and they'd descended into the world together. His interaction betrayed his lack of familiarity as he wandered into walls and she'd held his hand to keep him upright. But the virtual world wasn't for the faithful, according to his mother. Church remained the only virtual experience he'd had since that one day, when his mother had found the equipment and in no uncertain terms banished it from the house so that he didn't "turn out like your father."

A lengthy rubberized path led Joel between tall pecan and aspen trees, rustling as the wind tickled the leaves. Patches of bushes poked up along the walkway as he breathed in the clean air. A tiny hummingbird hovered near the honeydew bushes which had bloomed early. The bird's emerald green back and ruby-red throat shimmered in the sunlight. This could have been a sign to some, he thought. His mother would undoubtedly see the Lord's hand in it, as she always did with such simple things. It was beautiful, he admitted that as it captivated his interest and he watched it hover from the honeydew to a separating patch of Indian Blankets with their large bright orange flowers with red centers. He'd stepped into a painting.

A movement pulled his focus to the right, where native grasses had been reined in by thick cement boundaries. He sucked in his breath as his eyes fell on a man, hard at work clipping in the lower branches of an Oak tree that towered above the bluegrass. He recognized the thick red bush of hair and the beard, even if the man looked different without tears streaming down his pained face. When the hummingbird moved on, Joel's gaze stayed fixated on the man who was too intently wrapped up in his work to notice.

Until he wasn't.

Their eyes met, and the man smiled and waved genially toward Joel, who had no recourse but to return the greeting. When the man stopped his work and crossed the grass toward him, Joel froze in place. Too late to flee without insult, he'd been trapped by the man like a gazelle in the sight of a cheetah.

"Greetings young Mr. Joel." The man removed his gloves one after the other, and tucked them beneath his left armpit while extending his right hand for shaking.

"Praise to you, sir. I'm sorry, I don't know your name?"

"That's very proper of you, Mr. Joel," the man said with something of a smirk. "I'm Lonnie Lloyd. You can call me Lonnie though. Yer mother calls me Mr. Simpson, I suppose. Whatever works for you."

"Lonnie," Joel replied, feeling out the name with his lips. The man was one of those rare occasions where his name precisely matched his face, pudgy red cheeks and a bright red nose framed in red hair. Joel wasn't so fortunate. His dark brown skin and close-cropped hair — that would have been an afro left to its own will — often contradicted what people thought he would look like. New church members often let their eyes linger just a little longer once they met him.

"Praise be to you too, Mr. Joel," Lonnie followed up. "The Lord's morning is sure a beautiful thing. I'm so happy just to be here breathing the Lord's air and trimming the Lord's hedges."

"Not to be rude, but why haven't I seen you here before?"

"Mr. Joel?"

Joel considered whether he was mistaken in a moment of insecurity, but as he thought about it, his memory solidified. They did have a gardener, an elderly gentleman with thick glasses and who liked to call him Jolly, an ill-fitting description if there ever was one.

"What happened to the old gardener?"

"Sorry, Mr. Joel, I thought you knew? The Lord saw fit to take him from us last week, just after the Caitlyn woman."

The man's eyes began to mist over as though he'd know that man as intimately as a brother.

"How do you do that?"

"What's that, Mr. Joel?"

Joel took a deep breath and considered whether he wanted to harangue the man whose only crime so far was to introduce himself.

"Nothing, never mind. Nice to meet you."

"Mr. Joel, if there's a question to ask, I'll be honored to answer. Your mother is great with the Lord, and I'm guessing the Lord speaks through you too."

"It's just — at the funeral. You were there, right?"

To ask what Joel really wanted to ask meant revealing what he didn't feel. How do you feel the Lord so intensely that you carry on that way? What is it about me that makes me not be able to feel His presence?

"I was there for poor Ms. Parker," the man muttered in a solemn tone as he lowered his hand back to his side. "She went too young, too young. The Lord works in mysterious ways, and sometimes its a mystery to me as well."

"Amen to that."

"I know that we can't always understand the Lord, Mr. Joel. But your mother, she says that the Lord knows what he's doing and so I believe her. She knows why Ms. Parker had to die so early."

Joel wouldn't ask any questions. He couldn't take the chance to reveal himself to this man who he didn't know, and who seemed to know his mother.

"Thank you, Lonnie. It was a pleasure to meet you."

"Any time, Mr. Joel. I'll be here. Your mother was gracious enough to give me this job doing the Lord's work on these hedges."

The man slipped his thick gardening gloves back on and went back to his trimming, and Joel completed his morning stroll, more confused than ever about the world around him.

———

Breakfast with his mother brought the opportunity to learn a little more about Lonnie, and Joel thought he could work out some answers without arousing too much suspicion. He played at his eggs with his fork, turning them over before him as his mother devoured hers, doubtless running through her sermon in her head.

"Mom, when did you hire a new gardener?"

Her sharp eyes clipped over to his with that penetrating stare.

"I'm so sorry, Joel. I didn't want to tell you. Mr. Roy passed away a couple of weeks ago and, well, Mr. Simpson seemed so devout and so enthralled with the Lord, I thought that he's the perfect person to liven up the grounds here. Did you know he's been gardening professionally for years? He volunteers his time here. The man's practically a saint."

"We don't have enough money to pay him?"

"Joel, it's the Lord's money. The Lord wants us to use

that money to bring His word to the people. If we don't have to spend the Lord's money, then we shouldn't spend it."

"I was only asking a question."

Joel's mind popped back over to the shiny black luxury sedan his mother drove, but he said nothing.

"And there. I've answered it."

She went back to her bacon and eggs, scratching the fork with her knife.

"Couldn't we get a robot to do it?"

"Joel, it sounds like you don't like Mr. Simpson."

"That's not it, Mom. I met him this morning, and he seems nice enough."

She dropped her fork by her plate in a clang, and he saw her face slacken.

"You met him?"

"I went for a morning walk and he was out by the oak tree."

After a second pause, she spoke again.

"I guess that was inevitable. No, Joel, leave Mr. Simpson alone and let him do his work. He does the Lord's work, but he's had a hard life. It took him a long time to come to the Lord, and we don't want to mess up his life again."

"We just talked, Mom."

"I heard you. Just talked. I know. Just give him space, that's all I'm asking. Have you done the system check yet?"

"We just sat down to breakfast, Mom. Of course I haven't yet."

"Hurry over there after. It sounded a little tinny last night and some of the virtual viewers said there were glitches. Can you also check the virtual?"

"Fine, Mom. I'll check."

CHAPTER 5

WITH TWO HOURS TO go until the Sunday sermon was to begin, Joel fast-walked from their discrete house toward the chapel through the garden. He retraced a lot of the same steps from his morning walk, giving a wide birth to where he had met Lonnie. The dew still clung to some of the plants but the sun already beat down with an intensity that told him it would be a much warmer day than the day before. Passing through, he didn't see Lonnie or any of his gardening gear.

His heartbeat sped as he closed on the main building and pushed his way through the door. Joel knew the virtual system was working fine and that his check would be short. To be thorough, he had to submerge into virtual reality to hear the sermon playback the way she had, and that meant a possible few unsupervised minutes of exploration. As the door slammed shut behind him, he had already covered half the space to the engineer's booth. From there, he could run a quick diagnostic, and then move to the partially-hidden chamber behind the ready-room where the virtual reality troubleshooting rig lay tucked away.

Joel sat in the booth and pulled up the three-dimensional interface into the virtual reality hub, an interface that manifested as a solid slab that resembled what the refracting surface of ocean waves might look like pulled up into an obelisk. He stuck his hand into the intangible display and touched his index and thumb together. A series of spheres appeared in the mesh, carving out their own space in the scattered black and white static. Each tiny black dot represented a technology node in the virtual reality system. Touching each in order, they changed colors to indicate status. Green meant the device connected well and red meant there was trouble. All green. Joel flicked his fingers back apart and another set of bubbles rose into the ether. These were orange by design, and represented load. With no users online yet, orange was the appropriate color. Green would be a full virtual house and red would mean no traffic at all.

After the systems check, Joel closed his fist and the three-dimensional display fell into nothing. He made his way to the haptic rig, checking the time as he went. The check had taken only fifteen minutes, so he could easily have almost thirty minutes to check out virtual reality before people even began to arrive.

The haptic rig felt cramped as he pulled the pieces in. A few years old, the servos suffered from lack of use and the helmet visor had developed dead spots that jarred when in the virtual experience. Still, he slid into the gear, pulling it over his clothes. His mother would never buy a skin-to-skin suit that allowed indulging in all sorts of sinful acts, regardless of the improved virtual experience or the fact that he'd never at all indicated a predilection to such filth as online pornography. Gear like that would take at least an additional fifteen minutes just to put on anyway, and Joel would not be comfortable getting naked in the Lord's house, no matter how well the virtual chamber was hidden.

Joel first activated the sermon from the previous week. He saw the image of his mother standing taller than life on a stage made of porcelain. Fire skies flew by behind her, surrounding a cross in the heavens. He gasped at the imagery at first, having forgotten how intense the virtual experience hit on entry. The sky seemed to stretch up forever and made him imagine heaven shining down onto him. Even with the limited gear that he had, Joel felt the heat from the virtual light, God's light, on his skin. Then his rational brain kicked in and told him that this was all designed. They had the only interface like it in the world, being one of the wealthiest churches and having hired and paid top-dollar for the experience. But when it came down to it, the experience was just smoke and mirrors.

With a wave of disappointment, he shut down the sermon. Nothing strange happened there, it looked just as it was supposed to look — as he'd expected. The virtual system inspection never needed to be done and was only a distraction from further talk about Lonnie. The message couldn't be more clear — keep bringing Lonnie up, keep getting busy work. Don't talk about Lonnie. Curiosity welled within him and pushed against his brain, stifled with nowhere to go.

Joel pulled himself out of the sermon and flipped over to the virtual network with subvocal commands, issuing forth as little sound as possible in case his mother had descended early into the ready room to do her ritualistic preparation. He fell through an expanse of darkness and saw something that looked like a city with structures that resembled buildings. He landed with a solid thud beneath his feet, with just enough resistance to support himself, and looked around. The buildings rested beneath garish billboards, nearly half of which contained semi-nude or completely-nude women. Heat radiated through his body as his eyes fell on a fully-nude figure staring directly at him.

"Want to come in?" She mouthed the words seductively and then ran her left hand through her hair. The bar-code stamped on the inside of her left wrist was a promise that nothing was off-limits. Quickly he shifted his gaze away, down toward storefronts that promised more mundane things like virtual pets. Someone bumped him to the side, and he shrugged back, annoyed. The need for haptic feedback while navigating and searching for an experience seemed overkill to him. He jostled through the sea of people, most of whom would never remember seeing his avatar, a plain-looking man designed with modesty in mind. He pushed forward through the crowd, seeking the destination he knew awaited him while avoiding being swallowed up.

There were commands and subvocal that could get him there more quickly, but his apprehension mounted every second he waited, so he took the long way to avoid the risk of being overheard. As he approached his destination, the crowd began to thin and the tall, stark building rose before him — the search hub. Everything known to humans could be found in there, and it gathered more intelligence every day. He pushed his way in and executed the same search he always did. For this, he had to use his voice.

"Adisa Haines."

The interface pulled him upwards, flashing a tornado of images past too quickly to interpret. As the torrent slowed, he saw the one he wanted and reached out with his hands to grab it. A smiling man with dark brown eyes, almond skin and a thick bushy black beard came into focus. He felt his eyes start to water, but pushed that longing down. He wanted a hug — a long embrace so that he could smell his father's over-indulgent application of beard cleaner. Another image slammed into that one, a newer one. He pushed the first aside to look and sucked in his breath. The man now held a woman in his arms, someone who wasn't his mother, and who he'd never seen before. Sitting on her lap, a child rested, chubby and happy, wrapped up in the woman's arms.

"Exit."

He jerked back into reality and the darkness of the chamber. Quickly he pulled the helmet from his head and dropped it beside him on the floor. Tears streamed down his face unrelenting and a sob pushed its way across his lips.

Joel pulled the haptic suit free from his clothes and stood. From the sound of pacing, he knew his mother had finally made it into the ready room. With clumsy hands, he wiped at the tears and smeared them on his face. He had no mirror available, so he used his arm sleeve the best he could to get the rest of the ones he couldn't see, and made his way up to the ready room to greet her. With any luck, his mother would be too focused on her sermon to see the pain he felt.

He pushed his way through the door without knocking

"Mom, the virtual system is fine."

"Thanks, sweetie. Mommy's getting ready." She paused for a second. "Dallas County Revival is coming on Friday, dear. We need everything in tip top."

After dropping the bombshell, she dismissed Joel without even looking up. He barely registered that their competing megachurch would be in town. His father's happiness felt like a betrayal. He felt edgy and hurt. Joel stood in the doorway for a moment before leaving, silently debating whether it would be worth the inevitable fight to talk to her about his father again. He decided against it.

He emerged from the ready room ready to take his short walk to the engineer's box when his eyes landed on Delilah. He saw her face change from the bored look she normally wore in the sermons to a look of concern, prompting him to run his sleeve over his face once again just to be sure all the tears were gone. She still stared when his arm cleared his eyes, and she pushed her way toward the stage.

"Are you okay?"

The way she mouthed the words reminded him of the woman in virtual reality and he felt his face flush at the memory. Joel nodded briskly and took his place at the engineer's booth. Then the sermon began.

CHAPTER 6

AFTER THE SERMON, Delilah grabbed Joel on the way to Bible study, a surprise to him and from the look on her face, to her as well. Joel followed without complaint as she pulled him through a side door into an unused corridor.

"Are you really okay?"

Joel looked at her without answering her question straightaway, and considered his mother's sermon. The topic had been on infidelity, but not in the sense of man and wife. She'd expounded at length on loyalty to the church and through it to the Lord. Lonnie had done the bouncing and gyrating that Joel noticed every time now.

"I am," he told her, fighting a lump in his throat.

"Come on," she replied, pulling harder on his sleeve and taking him down the hallway he knew led directly to the garden outside. "You should see yourself, Joel. You're not okay. Talk to me about it."

Too tired to resist, Joel followed through a doorway out into the garden beneath the only willow tree on the property. The beaten-down and defeated tree still held onto a straggling of branches that whipped around when the wind hit it. She ducked as one of the branches swung around and caught Joel on the cheek. Delilah laughed when he felt the sting.

"Sorry, I don't mean to."

Her laugh broke his mood, and settled something inside of him. Joel couldn't stop the smile from cracking apart his lips. She sat on the bench under the sparse shade of the tree, and without prompting he sat beside her.

"Are you going to tell me?"

The desire to blurt out what had happened pushed against his stoicism, but for the moment, he tamped it back down into submission.

"Tell you what? I'm okay."

"Joel, your eyes looked like you'd been crying before sermon today. What happened?"

Joel took a deep breath as he considered whether he trusted her with the secret that he'd been on Labyrinth — a secret his mother couldn't know.

"I had to fix the virtual system today. Well not fix, look at it I guess. When I was in there, I ..."

He paused, looking at her, seeking understanding so he wouldn't have to confess. She only stared blankly back, not connecting his pause with meaning.

"I went into virtual reality."

"That's it?"

"I looked for my father in the search hub. And I found him."

"Oh."

The way she said it captured his attention, and he examined her face. The recognition was there — something about what he'd said she understood.

"He's happy. New family, new son, I think — still young.

He's got a new life, Delilah. And he's happy and smiling and enjoying himself and I'm..."

"Stuck here. With *her*."

Joel didn't acknowledge that statement. To acknowledge it would have been to admit that he feared his mother as much as he respected her, and wasn't happy here doing the Lord's work.

"I'm doing my duty to bring the Lord to the people, and he's abandoned even trying."

"Joel, your mother is a hard person. Life in this church is difficult. If you don't like it, you don't have to stay here. You don't *have* to like it."

"I want to do the Lord's work. And I want to be happy doing it. I don't understand what's wrong with me."

The words left before he had a chance to inspect them as he usually did, but they didn't scare him. To his surprise, relief followed in their wake.

"There's nothing wrong with you."

The sun broke through the clouds at that moment, and shot a ray down across her face. Her eyes glistened, wet with sadness as she looked at him beneath a furrowed brow. Delilah reminded him of Lonnie then, overwhelmed with the pain of everything that happened and so expressive about it. The sensitive soul who felt every wrong. Unlike Lonnie, Delilah's sadness was for Joel alone.

Then she hugged him.

At first, he didn't know why she pushed her way closer to him. Even when her arms went up, it had been so long since he'd hugged anyone that he didn't quite know what to do. As she pulled him in toward her, he felt that tug again in the back of his throat, and he couldn't keep it down. Joel planted his head in her neck and tears fell free, sliding down her shoulder, and as self-conscious as he felt about those tears finding their way over her body, he'd lost control. The sobs came out thick and heavy and with them, some of the pressure lifted.

Afterward, he pushed her away and stared at the dirt beneath the tree, starved of sunlight and bare and dusty.

"Joel, its okay."

He turned his head to face her and realized that she'd been crying too. Tears still ran down her cheek, tears from his pain. It was as if he'd given her some of his pain, cutting it out of himself and sewing it back into her somehow. Now she would carry his burden too.

"You're not used to opening up like this, are you?"

Of course not, he thought. Nobody opens up when their doing the Lord's work. It doesn't matter what he wants, but what the Lord wants. A Lord he couldn't hear. He shook his head.

"It's good to get it out sometimes," she told him, wiping her eyes. "It helps to share. You don't have to be alone."

Inside of himself, a seed seemed to have taken root. He felt something that he hadn't felt before. The tantalizing thought echoed through his body as a grin spread to his lips. That feeling, deep and warm and enticing, could only be one thing. He squeezed her hand as he stood, convinced that finally, after all of this time, he'd finally heard the Lord.

CHAPTER 7

JOEL FOUND himself in the garden the next day, near the same willow tree, searching through the sparse foliage for signs of Delilah's presence. He had no reason to believe that she would be there on a Monday. The weeks on the church grounds were mostly silent affairs, as the religious resigned themselves back to the humdrum activities of their normal lives and left the religiosity to the pious. The day's heat broke through late in the morning, lifting the dew from the flowers in steamy tendrils forking toward the sky. The bench was abandoned, though he made his way to it anyway, holding to the memory.

Leaves rustled nearby as the wind hit the aspens to his back. Turning slowly, hoping again for Delilah, he saw Lonnie, who waved and invited himself over.

"Nice day, Mr. Joel," the man told him, pulling his thick gardening gloves from his calloused hands. Joel felt the sensation of emptiness lowering itself over him with the man's presence, he being a constant reminder of the faith that Joel lacked.

"I suppose, Lonnie."

"It'll be a hot one too, if I'm not wrong."

"Probably."

The man didn't seem to catch onto the polite yet distant responses as a sign to leave, but he stopped talking and offered at least that peace. Instead, Lonnie seemed to take an interest in the willow branches, tracing them with his eyes. After about a minute, he lowered himself onto the bench and broke the silence.

"This tree was strong once," he said, pointing to a mottled spot on the trunk. "Then it took the sickness. Not much you can do once that sets in except watch it die. And trees kin take a long time to die. Sometimes years. But they're dying all the while."

"Joel?"

Joel's heart jumped as he turned his head toward the sound of Delilah's voice just beyond Lonnie's head. Lonnie shuffled a bit and rose to his feet slowly, holding his back as he emphasized the pain of the movement.

"I didn't think you'd be here," he said.

She smiled at him and then it didn't matter how pure Lonnie's love for the Lord seemed. Joel felt the deep warm sensation that filled his senses. Whatever Lonnie felt couldn't compare to that feeling. Delilah took Lonnie's place next to him and Lonnie stood for a moment, staring at the two of them together, then donned a quick smile and pulled his gloves back on.

"Who's the lady?" Lonnie asked the question directly to Joel, as though Delilah weren't even there. She spoke up before Joel could speak for her.

"I'm Delilah. What's your name?"

"Lonnie, Ms. Delilah. Lonnie Lloyd Simpson."

He bowed his head with a quick nod.

"It's a pleasure to meet you."

"Likewise, Ms. Delilah."

An awkward moment passed where again Lonnie stood in silence.

"The trees. They die slow."

Then Lonnie turned and walked off with long, sure strides that seemed incongruent with the painful way he'd risen to his feet. Delilah giggled once he was out of earshot.

"That guy is creepy."

"He feels the Lord."

"Maybe touched by the Lord is more like it."

"He seems off, but he feels the Lord. He was at Ms. Parker's funeral, and the only people that cried louder than him were her relatives. He was near you the other day at church. I've never seen anyone so moved."

"Anyone can wave their hands and speak in tongues, Joel. The Lord's got nothing to do with it."

His mother wouldn't agree with that. Joel shifted uneasily in his seat, until he felt her soft fingers across the back of his hand before they interwove with his own.

"I didn't mean to hurt you Joel. I worry about you sometimes. That mother of yours..."

"Don't talk about my mother, please."

She pulled her hand away and then rested it beside his instead, but he still felt the spark of electricity where her little finger touched his. From the corner of his eye, he watched her face shift downward and away from his, as a warm burst of air washed over his cheek.

When she looked down, he examined her face. Freckles dotted across the bridge of her nose. They gathered in clusters like blush circles on her cheeks and swooped down under her chin, accentuating its paleness with their presence. A strand of red hair swung before her tilted face, undulating with the wind before her right eye. His eyes followed over her arched eyebrows and thick eyelashes that extended out over pockets of eyeshadow. A bubbling feeling grew in his stomach as he watched her pinch her lips together then open them back apart again. He felt her pinkie rise and slide gently over his, pulling his attention down to their hands and the contrast of his dark skin tone over her pale pink-ivory.

That was when Joel realized that the feeling in his chest, heart, and entire body wasn't newfound joy in the Lord, but something else.

"Joel, I wanted to ask."

She tilted her head toward him and caressed his face with her green eyes.

"My mother and my dad, they want to have you over. Would you like to I mean if you're not too busy with the church... could you... come over for dinner on Thursday?"

Joels throat went dry and he closed his eyes, his first thought being that they would find out about his emptiness. The Reynolds, who had been over to his home often before his father left, rivaled his mother in devotion. They would surely see through him, pierce into him with their eyes and questions until the ugly truth rose out that he couldn't feel the Lord.

"You don't have to," she said, following up quickly.

"I can," he said in a low whisper. "I would love to."

Her smile irradiated warmth over him even as the churning in his belly grew more prominent.

———

He felt the first earthquake of his nerves when he walked in through the front door of their home. Usually left to fend for himself during the day, evenings were a different story. Dinner, as his mother constantly reminded him, was at six, and regardless of how *he* felt about it (his mother often skipped for various reasons). Skipping that half-hour to an hour long evaluation of his lack of progress toward the Lord reinforced his desire to go to Delilah's family for dinner instead. But he had to ask his mother to let him. He wasn't quite ready for the conversation when he discovered that his mother, who he'd expected to be working on her sermon in her study, was seated on the couch, still in her uniform. He tried the direct approach first.

"Mom, I can't make dinner tonight. The Reynold's have invited me over for dinner."

"Why would you want to go over there?"

"It's the Reynolds, Mom. We *used* to go visit them all the time when Dad was here. It's not a big deal."

He hadn't meant to mention his father. That was a certain way to make his mother dig into whatever positions she held, and as surely as he expected, she quickly leaned into her role as martyr.

"You mean your father who left me to raise you up to be a young man — *that* father. Listen, Joel, those people just — you can't trust them. I don't want you going."

Joel took a deep breath. He'd been through the routine many times, and he knew what it might take to get her to yes. But to do that, he would have to wade through the quagmire of guilt and shame that was coming next. He grit his teeth and looked away, steeling himself.

"What does it say in the Bible? Honor your father and mother, remember? *Honor*. You know that means you have to

...” She stalled out halfway through, perhaps registering that he was only superficially listening to her diatribe, or perhaps just to will out the tears that suddenly sparkled in her eyes. “You have to listen to me, don’t you? I don’t ask for much. A single mother, raising her little son. All I ask is that you be here at dinner. It’s a six o’clock. It’s time that we share together, and it’s important to me.”

“Mom, I’m old enough to be able to go have dinner at someone else’s house. I’m practically an adult.”

“And you’re going to leave me if I don’t let you. Is that what you’re saying? You’re going to leave me like *he* did. Here, alone, staring at my Bible.”

“I don’t understand you,” Joel said, raising his voice and feeling his stomach muscles contract as he did. “You ignore me like ninety-percent of the time. Even at dinner, it’s not like you *talk* to me.”

“I always talk,” she said, lowering her voice. “I’m the only one of us who does talk, Joel. I ask and ask but you don’t open up. It’s like you don’t want me to know anything about your life.”

She paused long enough to wipe a stray hair from across her forehead. Joel’s cheeks burned and he felt his breath quickening in his chest.

“The only time you ask me stuff is when I’m in the middle of either fixing the virtual reality equipment or doing something else. Dinner time you mostly ignore me and sit on your pinamu tablet.”

“Staying abreast of the news and protecting our family,” she said. “And you want to make me guilty for that? I *knew* you had too much of him in you. Faith isn’t something that he ever had, you know, that father of yours. I think he saw that in you, and that’s why he left. He left because he knew you couldn't be loved by the Lord. But I try, don't I? I try. And the thanks I get is you trying to leave?"

Joel bit his lower lip until he tasted salt, trying to stay the fury that welled beneath the surface of his skin. He stared at her until the scorching flames of hatred passed, only to have them resolve into a feeling of which he was intimately familiar — self-loathing. Who was he to want anything anyway? And had Delilah really even wanted him over, or was she just being nice to the heir of the church — playing him for a fool?

No. As he thought of Delilah, he thought of her touch across the palm of his hand. He focused on her green eyes locked into his dark brown ones, and a smile so genuine that he couldn't have doubted it if he tried.

"No, Mom. This isn't about me, and it's not a lot to ask. Just one night with Delilah — I mean, at the Reynolds — for dinner. That's it. If you want, I'm sure they'll let you come."

"To those evil people," she hissed. "And that Jezebel who's trying to steal my son from me? The Lord strike me down before I let you go with *them*."

He stood, amazed at his ability to do so. The voice still rang inside of him, telling him that he wasn't worthy of the Lord's love, and it was no wonder he couldn't feel it. He was too much like his father. He'd been the reason that his father left. Joel sucked in a deep breath and latched onto the one good thought that he could find: Delilah *wanted* him there. He forced a smile to show that his mother wasn't getting to him, even though she'd stripped him bare and exposed every insecurity that he'd kept bottled inside.

"I'm going," he announced. Her immediate reaction was to clamp her mouth together and then glare. "I don't know why we stopped seeing them in the first place. I *remember* when we used to go over there and they came over here. Dad, you, Mr. and Mrs. Reynolds, and Delilah — all of us. We had fun and sang Psalms, even the ones that don't rhyme. I remember the chocolate chip cookies we always ate afterwards, and the taste of them soaked in fruit punch like Delilah and I *always* did. I remember all of that. They're not enemies, Mom. It's not fair to call them that."

"So," she whispered through clenched teeth. "You made up your mind."

Joel swallowed but nodded in resolution and clenched his hands to help draw together what strength he could find.

"I guess there's nothing else to talk about then," she said.

It wasn't a yes, but it *was* as close as he would get. She turned away and left him stranded, alone. The plush greens and purples of the opalescent curtains and the remains of sunlight that streamed that bounced off of them to hue the room seemed to mock him as her rapid departure made the curtains swing and send flickers around the living room. He crumbled then, falling to the couch with a thud, acknowledging to himself that he had only won the bought, but he would pay. Somehow, when he didn't expect it, she would use this against him too. He didn't know if it was worth it, but he did relish the thought of seeing Delilah again.

Later that evening, he pulled on his less formal blazer and slacks, leaving his official clothes in favor of the more casual, and with a shaky heart, made his way out the front door accompanied only by the sound of his mother's relentless sobs emanating from behind her locked bedroom door.

CHAPTER 8

IN APRIL, the days stretched over twelve hours long so the sun rested just above the evening's horizon casting shadows across the garden. Joel crossed to make his way to Delilah's house. The cicadas began early and rose with their deafening chorus, blotting out all other sounds except the dull thud of his shoes against the cemented walkway. Upon leaving church grounds, Joel easily found his way along the suburban streets to the home he recognized from his memory, a large two-story building with pillars in the front and three vehicles in the driveway that rivaled his mother's in cost. As he neared the door, it popped open to welcome him in, doubtless pre-programmed to open on his biometric signature as a greeting.

"Come in, Joel, hun." A tall woman whose eyes matched Delilah's smiled at him as he entered. She couldn't have been waiting for him, but somehow she met him in the entryway just as he passed through. "Let me take your coat."

"Yes, ma'am."

"No need for that here. We're practically family. You

remember, don't ya? Your father is such a good man. Did I tell you he's the reason we came to this church in the first place?"

"Mary, let him alone. He just got here."

"Dad, Mom, I've got it."

Delilah swung around the corner smiling at Joel, and grabbed the blazer that he'd already begun to hand to her mother and shepherded it to a closet near the foyer. Then she turned as quickly to grab his hand and pull him through the house. He followed in tow, careful to smile at each of her siblings as they passed by.

The table that she seated him at extended long enough to seat eight people. There was enough room for twelve if they were sitting elbow-to-elbow. She pointed him to a seat near the head of the table, and plopped down by his side.

"They can be a bit nosey," she warned. "Don't worry, they just want to know about you, and how you're doing, that's all."

"And how is he doing?" Her father's voice boomed in from the kitchen doorway.

"Fine, sir. I'm doing fine."

"Joel, we're great friends of your father — such a good man. We're sorry about all that mess that happened when he left, really."

Only bits of the story had survived Joel's childhood to embed themselves in his conscious memory. Vague recollections of screaming and constant tension in their home combined to layer over all of his childhood memories.

"Dad, leave it alone. I'm sure Joel doesn't want to rehash all of that stuff."

Joel realized when she squeezed that she'd never let go of his hand, and he smiled at her.

"Joel, if you want to talk about it but Delilah's stopping you, blink twice. I think it's a crime how little you were told."

"Dad, I told you."

"I'll drop it, really this time."

"Delilah, I could use some help in here," Delilah's mother's voice echoed from the kitchen. Delilah shot a warning glare toward her father before she rose from the table to make her way into the kitchen. Her father made his way over to the table and sat down at the head.

"I guess if we can't talk about your father, we'll have to talk about Delilah," the man said, smiling a warm permeating smile. His thick dark-reddish-brown hair made Delilah's seem tame, and the man's skin was nearly alabaster-white. Without Delilah's mother and her tan complexion mixed in, Joel considered that Delilah might have ended up albino.

"About Delilah, sir?"

"How do you feel about her?"

The question prompted Joel to introspect and wade through his emotional landscape. He felt safe with her, even now, with the ever present fear of discovery under prying questions and eyes, he felt that at least one person in the entire world wouldn't care about that. His heart rose in his chest as he tried to imagine the conversation where he confessed to Delilah that he couldn't feel the Lord. She would laugh. "So what?" She would say. How to put that feeling into words completely escaped him, and he wasn't sure that her father would understand anyway.

"Don't say anything, Joel. I can see it all over your face. You have to know that she feels the same way about you. I can't get her to shut up."

The man laughed and stuck out his hand.

"Pleased to meet you, Joel."

Joel shook his hand without understanding much of what was happening. Delilah's father pulled him in close and whispered at him.

"Now, just keep that between us. I don't think Delilah wants you to know yet that she likes you."

Likes you. Delilah had used those words before, but not the way her father did. Delilah actually liked him, deficient in faith and failure that he was. As his thoughts turned back to Delilah, she entered the room as though he'd willed her there. She met his eyes and smiled, then placed a pan of something that he didn't care to look at on the table before him, brushing his arm with her elbow in the process, before re-taking her seat.

"Are you okay?"

"Y-yeah."

Dinner with the Reynolds was unlike any dinner he could remember. The conversation flowed effortlessly from person to person, and aside from a few cursory conversations about the weather and work that went into preparing for the sermons. At least, dinner began amiably enough. After a couple of glasses of wine, Delilah's mother maneuvered the conversation around to the topic of Joel's father.

"It was strange how he left," she said.

"Mom!"

"No it's fine, I won't say much. Just that running off in the middle of the night like that. What was the point of all the dramatics? I'd known him since... Jonathan, how long do you think we were friends?"

"Since childhood, you always say."

"Right. The least he could have done was let me know he was going. You'd think that when your best friend is going to disappear, they'll tell you about it first."

A whir came from the kitchen doorway as a MiniMaid robot came through the door and began collecting empty dishes from the table with its vice-like pinchers.

"We kissed once, did you know that?"

"When they were in the third grade," Delilah's father added. "It was cute. I think there's a picture around here somewhere."

"Mom. Dad. Stop it," Delilah said. Her little brother and sister whispered to each other and giggled.

"It's just so strange that he would leave like that."

"Mary, maybe we should drop the subject."

"Fine. I'll drop it. Just, that mother of yours."

"Mom, let it go."

"I'll have some more wine."

After dinner, Delilah walked Joel to the door to say good-bye. As she retrieved his coat from the front closet, she apologized profusely for her parents.

"They get gooey when they drink. I complain, but they don't care."

"It didn't bother me," Joel said. A prickling sensation tickled the back of his mind as he knew that he needed to know more. Not just about his father, but he also needed to know about how a family can joke like that, have fun, even argue, and all as natural as breathing. Asking about that would make him seem even stranger than he already did, so he resorted to the topic of his father instead.

"Was there something strange about my father leaving? Aside from, you know, his leaving."

Joel accepted the blazer and pulled it over his arms.

"Not the way they make it out to be, like some sort of nefarious scheme. I don't know what that's about."

He buttoned the bottom two buttons on his jacket.

"Thank you for inviting me."

"You're welcome."

Before he knew what was happening, she pushed herself up to him and gave him a kiss on the lips, soft and gentle, and gone before he knew it was even there.

"Thank you," she whispered as she pulled away from him. As he backed up, pondering the kiss and what it meant, the door picked up his biometric signature again, swung inward and pushed him into her arms, where she kissed him again. This one was longer and this time, he wrapped his arms around her and kissed her back.

Moments later, he made his way down the sidewalk, replaying both kisses in his mind and smiling with no one to witness.

CHAPTER 9

FRIDAY NIGHT, Dallas County Revival arrived in town. They had no reason to be in Austin except to steal parishioners away from his mother. Competing churches did that from time to time — well, all but Austin Life Community. Joel's mother considered such things offensive to the Lord and wouldn't participate in sniping at other congregations. On the other hand, Dallas County Revival, with their pastor Franklin Thomas, held one of their namesake revivals only eight blocks away from the doors of Austin Life. Not only did this get Dallas County Revival on the news, but it also got them an invitation to dinner by his mother, who believed firmly in keeping enemies close.

"Why do we have to have them here?" Joel asked Lonnie the question as though Lonnie would know something that he didn't about it. Lonnie only smiled and pulled chairs out as the prepared the hall for their guests.

"The Lord knows."

"Have you seen his sermons? His virtual avatar looks like he's wrapped in a white bubble. It's horrible."

The man had slicked back hair and a greasy smile that always set Joel's nerves on edge. This wasn't the first time that Pastor Franklin had been to their church but each time Joel hoped would be the last. Even though his mother had told Joel not to get too close to Lonnie, Joel recognized that Lonnie had to do all of the setup work by himself and wasn't going to let him do it alone. Lonnie shouldn't have had to place down chairs by hand in the big hall anyway, as far as Joel was concerned. With all of the money the church made, they could afford robots or even androids to do the work, but the Lord needs his money more than they need robots, according to his mother, in her designer heels.

Honor thy mother.

The words materialized in his mind as he felt the guilt of his judgment. Why shouldn't she have nice shoes? The shoes didn't cost anywhere near the price of an android anyway, and work builds character. There was a message in his work about the Lord, if he could only listen for it. Then, in the faintest whisper, he felt something that he thought might finally be the Lord's work. A question stemmed in the back of his mind and he turned it over and over, looking at it. The question was for Lonnie. If Lonnie could feel the Lord, why couldn't he?

"Lonnie," Joel began, placing a chair down and sliding it beneath a lengthy silver banquet table. Lonnie immediately stopped what he did and stared at Joel, awaiting further instruction and reminding him of a mechanized worker.

"How is it that you feel the Lord so much?"

"The Lord in His kindness has seen fit to bless me with a keen sense of emotion, Mr. Joel. The Lord works in mysterious ways."

"I don't understand. You didn't even know that woman from the week before, did you?"

"I knew her and of her. The Lord called her to Him too soon."

Even now, after over a week, Lonnie's eyes teared up over it.

"I feel sad, Lonnie. I feel terrible that it happened to her, and I was just with Ms. Parker not too long ago. But I didn't cry, not once. You cried so much I'm pretty sure you ran out of tears."

"People need somebody to miss them, Mr. Joel. I miss them for you, and everyone else. I miss them so you don't have to. The Lord tells me to."

Joel slid the chair into place and went to a stack by the wall to retrieve another.

"The Lord tells you to cry?"

"He tells me to cry and beat my chest and gnash my teeth. He does, the perfect and terrible Lord. But that's not all He tells me."

The man said the words in such an unexcited manner that to Joel, it was as if commenting on the sky. "The clouds are white and the Lord speaks to me." He felt jealousy grow in his heart, and tried his hardest to push it back down, thinking of Cain and Abel, and the terrible mark that jealousy had left on the world. Joel slid that seat into place and went for another.

"The Lord told me there'd be another death soon," said Lonnie.

At that, Joel's ears perked up and he turned to face Lonnie, dropping the next chair in place. He winced as it landed on his foot and then slid down beside it onto the ground.

"What did you say?"

"I said the Lord tells me stuff."

"After that."

"There'll be more dying soon. This is something that the Lord has said."

"As in the Lord, Lord?" Joel pointed a finger into the sky.

"Soon. You'll see."

The way he said it, with a twinkle in his left eye like he would enjoy wailing over yet another coffin, made Joel clench his teeth. He regretted not taking his mother's advice and staying away from Lonnie at that moment. The man clearly was insane.

But who was Joel to question? He'd never heard the Lord or even felt Him. The Lord could move in such ways, couldn't He? Was Joel so important that if the Lord didn't talk to *him*, He couldn't talk to Lonnie and tell him things like when people would die? He gulped down his pride and slid the chair into place. They only had five left to move, so Joel grabbed one more and pulled it to the table.

"Tomorrow. That'll be the day."

Now the man was getting too specific. Joel resisted the urge to say anything and pushed the chair under the table. It was time to change the subject.

"Do you have any family, Lonnie?"

Lonnie paused with his work and looked at Joel as though he were thinking.

"The good Lord hasn't seen fit to bless me with any. He took my son Jonah away from me early. Him, my wife and our daughter Jenna, may they rest with the Lord."

"What happened?"

"They were staying downtown in League City when the shooting happened. Wrong place, wrong time. I was picking up doughnuts at Besties Bakery on 1ˢᵗ avenue. Jonah wanted one the size of his head."

Lonnie smiled as he held up his hands in a circle in front of his face.

"This big. Jenna wanted the Unicorn Sparkle. Debrah — my wife — she was on a diet, but still couldn't resist an old-fashioned."

The man's gleaming eyes and widened smile seemed to celebrate rather than mourn. If the Lord wanted Lonnie's children, then Lonnie would have given them willingly, Joel thought.

"I'm sorry."

"The Lord called them to Him, that's all. It was time, and I was blessed to have them for as long as I did."

Lonnie slid the last chair in place, and they both looked at the long table. Over fifty chairs seated around a great monstrosity in the middle of the hall. In a few hours, those chairs would be overflowing with select parishioners from the two churches who had paid more than twenty-thousand dollars per chair to attend. And Joel already knew that none of those chairs would be empty. Three were reserved for Delilah and her parents. He laughed at the mental image of Delilah in her Sunday best wedged in between his mother and Franklin Thomas.

"Whatcha laughing about?"

Even without a hint of anger in the man's voice, the inappropriateness of the moment made Joel queasy. He restored a stoic blank face.

"I'm sorry, Lonnie. I didn't mean to laugh, and it wasn't about your tragic situation. Please forgive me."

"Like I said, the Lord called them. No forgiving needed, Joel."

"I've got to go get ready, Lonnie. My mom is waiting. Are you joining us tonight?"

"No Mr. — Joel, I mean. The Lord has other plans for me."

Half an hour later, the dinner hall overflowed with party goers and Lonnie disappeared. Members from each congregation seemed like old friends, chatting about scripture and the weather, the two main points that it was always safe to discuss. Joel's mother and Franklin sat side-by-side at the table, with their parishioners around them. As Joel approached to take his seat among them, beside where Delilah sat with her family, his mother spoke.

"Would you mind keeping an eye on the children's table, Joel? Someone has to look after them and we don't have anyone else."

Joel met Delilah's eyes for a moment before resigning himself to obey.

"I will, Mom."

"Thank you, Joel. It must have slipped my mind to get someone to look after them."

Delilah whispered something to her mother, who glanced up toward Joel and then back to Delilah before nodding.

"I'll come too, Joel," she told him, and stood from the table. He didn't have to look to his mother to know that she scowled at that. Joel couldn't figure out what it was about Delilah that the woman hated so. He smiled at Delilah as she came to join him, and she touched him lightly on the shoulder with her fingertips, a feeling that lingered all the way to where the children sat.

The pair sat at the children's table, and Joel was so focused watching Delilah play games to entertain the children that he lost that sense of irritation that he'd first had at his mother's command.

"Ms. Delilah, can you do a reindeer?"

Her hands shot up to the sides of her head and she tilted her head back.

"You have to fly!" One little boy's voice rose above the clammer, and Delilah jumped to her feet and sprinted around the table, causing the little boy to jump up and chase her. Joel almost joined in but would have felt too ridiculous following them around.

"Joel," he heard a whisper at his back, and turned to see who it was. Delilah's mother stood over him. "I'll watch them. You and Delilah go do things. You shouldn't have to be here for this."

Delilah slowed as she came back around to where her mother stood. Then she smiled broadly.

"Thanks, Mom, you're the best."

She gave her mother a hug. Joel watched the pair examine each other displaying the fondness he would expect in any family with genuine, thoughtful looks and smiles. He basked in their warmth.

"Let's go," Delilah said to Joel, and grabbed his hand before he'd even stood, pulling him away and toward the exit door. Joel cast a look over his shoulder toward his mother, but she busily entertained her guests.

A few minutes later, they emerged out into the garden still hand in hand. Joel felt his palm grow sweaty and, conflicted about whether the sweat would bother her, fidgeted with his fingers until she clamped down and stilled his worry.

"It's so beautiful here," she told him, and when she said it he saw it. The trees were vibrant green, and even the thick oaks with all of their mystery changed from creepy to majestic with her words.

"Where do you want to go?" He asked as she led him along the trails, back to the very same bench that they'd sat at together when she consoled him before. She led him to the seat, and he joined her, afraid to let go of her hand in case he should never get it back.

His heart pounded in his chest and he felt his stomach harden, clenched with anticipation. Joel looked at her, outlined in a halo of light, and she looked at him. Inch by inch, they pushed closer to each other until her nose nearly touched his. Then, without warning, she kissed him.

It wasn't like the time before. This time, the kiss lasted longer than a peck, and her lips lingered against his even when it was done while she sucked in air to kiss him again. He returned her passion, licking his lips and leaning forward, pressing himself into her, seeking her tongue. The smell of her was all around him, blotting out his world and sucking him in. That feeling returned, the one of that he'd thought at first was the Lord, but he'd been right. It was her, producing some sort of miracle around him, curing his world.

"Mr. Joel, does your mom know you're out here?"

He pulled back quickly from her and turned to see Lonnie, leaning on a shovel and grinning at him broadly. Grinning and staring, but less at him now that he noticed. Lonnie had fixated his gaze on Delilah this time.

"Don't tell her, please," he replied, faster than he could think.

"What?" Delilah complained to him. "Why would you not want your mother to know about me?"

"That's not what I meant."

"That's what I heard," Lonnie chimed in, not helping.

"I just mean I don't know how she'd react. She's weird about some things."

"Like making out at a church gathering?" He noticed then that Delilah smiled when she said it, and she probably had been the entire time.

"Oh, you're joking."

Lonnie and Delilah both laughed.

"You really had him going," Lonnie said.

"You started it with your comments there, Mr. Simpson."

"I like you, girl."

Joel felt a fire burn in his gut and spread out to his cheeks. He pulled his hand from Delilah's and felt his cheeks flush in hot bursts, and the laughter continued. Delilah's voice broke free.

"Joel, I was only teasing. Lonnie won't tell anybody, especially not your mother."

"Of course he will. You don't understand."

"I won't, Mr. Joel. That's between you young ones and the Lord."

"Don't talk to me about the Lord right now." Joel's voice came out as a torrent of scalding words that fell around him, washing over Lonnie and Delilah both. He hadn't meant to sound that way, like he might at any moment tear someone's esophagus free from their necks, but the sharpness of his voice couldn't be denied. Silence settled over them all. As he looked to Delilah, he saw her eyes wide and mouth shut tightly, with her jaws clenched together.

"Mr. Joel, are you okay?"

"Leave me alone, Lonnie."

Joel fled. He staggered off in embarrassing form, nearly tripping over a lip between two cement panels, which aggravated him further. He lost himself in the garden, careful to avoid any areas he thought his mother might be.

As he stormed his way to his room, his only thought was that he should have known better than to trust. Once hidden, Joel spent hours in darkness. When his mother finally crashed through the front door, he listened in silence to her traipsing about after she returned from her dinner, not bothering to find out if he was okay at all. He wouldn't have told her anyway, after the humiliation he'd suffered.

Like Job, Joel suffered in the battle between the Lord and the Devil. And like Job, the questions sprang into his heart. Had the Lord abandoned him because he was weak and unworthy? Why would such miseries of existence be heaped upon someone whose only desire was to feel his love?

But it wasn't. Even as Joel formed the words, he felt Delilah's lips across his own, her probing tongue and the smell of her sweat mingling with his. In that vision, deep in his mind, they writhed together like snakes among his sheets, naked and glistening. He pushed at the image, struggled with it, forced it to go, but it always returned. There was no God in that mass of bodies in his imagination, only sin.

Maybe he was Job. If so, Delilah was either a gift or a test. In the shadow of the Lord's disregard, could Joel be the island that stood firm, resisting temptation and staying the chosen course, even if he suffered from loneliness, hopelessness, and pain. Perhaps, just maybe, if Joel can persevere like the man from whom everything was stolen away, then Joel would get blessings of a thousand times what he'd lost. But if those blessings came without Delilah, he wouldn't want them.

The force of Delilah's kiss re-emerged, crushing him to his knees. The passion behind it overwhelmed his senses, but this time, to coat the temptation with cruelty, she exposed her smile to him. There was no nudity, no writhing bodies, but in their stead, only her. She wore her Sunday dress that she'd worn that day, and smiled at him. That was the extent of it, a smile that told him that she accepted him, that she could see herself loving a man like him. The lie of a smile before she'd conspired to make a fool of him. But he couldn't lie to himself. If the Lord would give him a thousand blessings for his sufferings, then she must be one.

And the other one of the only two blessings he would ever need to walk this road into night was the blessing of his father back, only not today, but years ago. Instead of leaving, Joel would have him there to play ball with, to watch Zephyr matches with and slip him little drinks of beer at the games so that he would know he was normal. Joel's mother would still love the man, and that love would inevitably include Joel, because it had to. The three of them, talking the way Delilah and her parents talked, teasing each other for silly reasons, and not being hurt by the words.

His eyes were dry.

The tears didn't fall, nor did they want to. The pain had evolved into numbness, and now he lay staring into the black.

If the Lord required him to be Job, the eternal sufferer, then he would be Job.

CHAPTER 10

SATURDAY AFTER CHURCH, Joel skipped Bible study and made his way back into the garden again — this time without Delilah. The garden seemed dreary and bleak without her despite the overwhelming sun already saturating the leaves. Joel found himself drawn to the bench where he and Delilah had sat before under the diseased willow tree.

"Where's your girlfriend?" Lonnie's voice caught Joel as he was about to lower himself to it.

"She's not my girlfriend. It doesn't matter."

"Here."

Lonnie handed a set of sheers over to Joel, who went to work on the hedges, carefully clipping each section until each branch was exactly the same length. He worked at a slow, deliberate pace, focusing on the work and ignoring any deviations of his mind. The Lord willed him to do yard work. The thought was asinine, but here he was.

"You're not gonna tell me, Mr. Joel?"

"Joel. Listen Lonnie, it's Joel. It will always just be Joel."

"You're not gonna tell me, Joel?"

"You won't be seeing her again, Lonnie. It's just me."

With that he finished one hedge, and tossed the shears down to the dirt beside the cement. Joel took several quick paces toward the church building, and burst in through a side door. He felt the chill of the climate-controlled inner sanctum as he pivoted toward the bathroom. Then he pushed through the doors and stepped up to a stall to piss. About halfway through, the sound of the door opening behind him diverted his attention. He grunted an acknowledgement without turning around, finished up, then zipped his pants. Joel turned around and stopped when he saw a reflection in the mirror. Delilah smiled sheepishly in the mirror at him. He turned angrily toward her.

"What are you doing in here?"

"You weren't at Bible study. Lonnie said you'd come this way and I made a guess."

"This is the men's room, right?"

"Just a bathroom, Joel. I need to ask you something."

Joel tried to focus on washing his hands, and shoved them underneath the automatic faucet.

"Need soap?"

He pulled a hand free from the water, dropped soap into it, and then shoved it back in.

"Joel, what happened yesterday? You got pissed and then ran off. Did I do something?"

"I can't be with you," he told her, jaw set in determination. "This can't happen. I want to, but I can't. The Lord wants something different for me."

Her face fell and her eyes drifted away from him. She suddenly seemed helpless and frail in the reflection, and part of him wanted to take it back. But the Lord demands what the Lord demands. Her face stayed flat for a second, then twisted up into a scowl.

"The Lord wants, Joel? The Lord? Or is it your mother?"

"It's not my mother. Not everything about me has anything to do with my mother."

Probably a lie.

"Just tell me, Joel. Do you feel what I feel? Do you ache every moment we're apart, like a piece of you has been cut off and you can't find it until you're with another?"

"Of course, Delilah. You tempt me like no one else could. I've had..."

He stopped short of telling her what he'd been fighting against the evening before.

"What?"

Joel looked at her in the mirror and then resigned himself to his fate, turning to face her directly. He had to be strong, like Job.

"Impure thoughts," he muttered, then quickly followed. "I can't sleep at night. I can't even think."

The embarrassment couldn't actually be seen on his dark cheeks, but Joel could feel them burning. She had to understand that, he didn't want to say more.

"That's all? That's what's got you all messed up? I told you it was your mother. I didn't know it was this bad or I wouldn't even have bothered."

"Bothered with what? Never mind. Move out of my way, Delilah."

He glared at her, pasting on the expression so that she could see he was serious, though the face ran counter to the longings in his heart. Temptation had to be more than avoided — it had to be rejected outright. *She* had to be rejected.

"I'll move when you tell me the truth. Do you love me?"

Joel stormed toward her and let fly the words he already knew he'd regret.

"You are temptation."

Delilah stepped to the side as he stomped toward her, and let himself out through the door. He froze in the hallway and listened to the slow swing of the door back to closing. The air had been sucked out of him and his stomach dropped. Thirty seconds later, he still couldn't move, and Delilah still hadn't emerged. He crossed through the door back out into the garden where Lonnie stood there grinning like an idiot.

"She came back."

Joel didn't say another word. Instead, he turned again and made his way back into the church, and hid himself in the ready room. Nobody would be in there for the rest of the day. He could sulk and be miserable alone, just as he used to before Delilah, and as he would again get used to after her. Yet somehow, the stabbing pain in his chest wouldn't subside. And, somehow, Lonnie found him only after about ten minutes.

"Mr. Joel," Lonnie began, and Joel didn't correct him. "You asked me how I feel the Lord."

Joel looked at him with a blank stare, unsure that there was anything Lonnie might say that could change his fate. Lonely and alone would be his future.

"It's easy, Mr. Joel. I mean, Joel. It's real easy. All you have to do is do the Lord's work."

The man's words meant nothing, but his smile was genuine and Joel felt that Lonnie sincerely wanted Joel to feel better, so he managed a weak grin.

"Really?"

"You've been helping me with the garden, and that's part of it. But there's more, too."

"What?"

"I can't tell you yet. But you keep helping me in the garden, and I'll show you soon, I promise. Don't fear, Joel. There's always hope, especially for you."

———

That evening, more than the impure thoughts kept Joel awake. Now his nemesis consisted of impure thoughts and the vague idea that he would never have another basis for those impure thoughts again. Never would he have another kiss from her to fuel his sleepless nights. This idea poked at him every time he closed his eyes for sleep.

Tossing and turning, at just after midnight, Joel gave up. He threw on his sandals, a warm overcoat — the only piece of his father's clothing that his mother had let him keep, and set out into the darkness of the evening. His mother wouldn't be awake for hours.

The night sky revealed the sparse whiskers of the Milky Way galaxy, spread out over the heavens by a star-brush. The moon rested just above the horizon, and the gentle sounds of cicadas echoed through the night. But that wasn't all he heard in the sound. A whimper rode atop the background noise, like a wounded animal. Thinking it might be a deer, as they wander into the garden from time to time, he made his way through the thick trees toward where the sound originated.

Joel followed the cement trail through the garden as he had so many times before, turning left and right as the trail demanded, but always toward the sound. He didn't know what he might do when he got there — perhaps call animal control, he considered. Whatever animal he found would doubtlessly bite him only to drive home the lesson of what his life is meant to be. The closer he got, the more overtones he was able to discern, and the sound began to morph from a scavenging rodent to something a lot larger than raccoon. By the guttural growls and subsequent whimpers, he began to think that the animal might be a coyote or a wolf, so slowed his gait. A small gardener's shed appeared on the path before him.

Joel paused for a second to get his bearing on the sound again. It seemed to come from the shed, strange because the door was usually locked tight. Joel neared the door and paused, telling himself that if he needed to run, the nearest tree was only a few feet away. He imagined himself running toward the tree and grabbing the first few branches to swing upward to safety. Joel could do that.

But first, he needed to open the door so whatever was in there could get out. The door was shut tight, but the padlock swung loose. He pulled it off without thinking, only to have the thought occur once he had the door in full swing. The lock may not have been bolted, but it was definitely in the latch. No animal could have gotten in that building with the door shut as it was. When he stepped into the room, his eyes took a second to adjust to the dim lighting.

Joel blinked rapidly to clear his confused eyes, but the scene before him stayed. There, tied to a table before him, struggling against restraints, he caught the wild eyes of Franklin Thomas staring out over a gag. In shock, Joel only stood and stared while the man pleaded at him with his eyes to set him free. Then, Joel heard the sound of breathing behind him.

Joel's pulse raced and he could feel the sensation in his ears. His jaw seized up and his entire body froze.

"Mr. Joel, did you come to help?"

"H-help?" Joel whispered through clenched teeth.

"I'm guessing the Lord sent you to help with this work. That's good, it can be lonely sometimes. Can you grab that needle over there?"

Joel didn't move.

"Never mind, I'll get it."

Lonnie stepped around Joel and toward the needle. Within it swirled a dark blue fluid that Joel didn't recognize. His mind raced — he should intervene. Whatever Lonnie said, the Lord wouldn't want this work. Would he? Joel wouldn't know.

"What are you doing?" He finally forced the words out through his lips.

"Killing Mr. Franklin here. This paean is guilty in the eyes of the Lord."

"Paean?"

All of his words came out in question form, when what he really wanted to do was to shout at the man to stop, but he still couldn't move.

"Offering to the Lord, Joel, it's not complicated. This paean is a child molester, someone who deserves the Lord's wrath for what he did to those innocents in his congregation."

Joel felt his jaw slacken as he grappled with whether he should intervene with a child molester's death. The Lord worked in mysterious ways, and Joel didn't interfere as the needle penetrated the man's neck, nor as the fluid drained slowly into the man's body. Joel's feet still wouldn't move and he couldn't look away as the darting of the man's eyes came to a slow stop, the man staring blankly up toward the ceiling.

"If you're not gonna help, you may as well leave," Lonnie grunted at him as he pulled the straps to release the man.

A lifeless arm fell dow beside the table, and that seemed to break the spell. Joel backed through the open door behind him and turned, attempted to catch his breath but couldn't. One more deep pull through his teeth and the air moved again. He pushed his legs to move too, one before the other, as he teetered through the doorway and towards the main church building.

"M-m-m..." Joel tried to call his mother, but the words wouldn't come out. Lumbering forward like a mute zombie, he covered the cement walkway quickly, and ducked into the hallway, slamming the door behind him.

What had he just witnessed? He took off down the hallway and made his way through the church to their living quarters, and then thankfully to his room without coming across his mother. Through the door and into the safety of his sanctuary, Joel slumped down, back against the door. Two knocks sounded out behind him and he jumped, then clenched his teeth down. He hadn't come in unnoticed after all.

"Joel, are you in there?"

"Leave me alone, Mom."

"I'm not going to do that, Joel. Open the door or I will."

He jumped to his feet, feeling rage course through him. He needed a few moments of quiet and peace, and even that would be denied him. The door creaked open behind him and he didn't turn to look at her.

"Are you okay, honey?"

"I'm fine."

"Is there anything you want to talk about?"

A question occurred to him then.

"Franklin Thomas," he said. "Was he a child molester?"

"Wh — who told you that?"

"It doesn't matter. Was he?"

He turned to watch her face, even though she was a much more accomplished liar than he. Still he locked into her eyes as she seemed to consider her response.

"It depends. A parishioner is accusing him, you probably know. The statute of limitations has expired though. Franklin brought it up tonight. He said he's innocent so I guess only the Lord knows. Why?"

"Lonnie said he was. I just hadn't heard that before."

Her face flashed at the mention of Lonnie. Just to confirm what he'd seen, Joel continued.

"I saw him in the garden today."

"When?"

"Just now. I was out walking a moment ago. I thought you heard me come in."

Her face flashed again, like a hint of fear and then it was gone.

"Did he say anything else?"

"He said he does the Lord's work."

She gulped at that but said nothing. Instead she tried to change the subject.

"You can talk to me about it, if you want. I know you're going through some things right now."

He resisted the urge to say that he had been talking to her, and she'd just essentially told him to stop by changing the subject. Instead, he nodded in silence, and took a seat on his bed, counting the minutes until she got tired of playing mother and either became angry and hurled insults at him, or left him in a huff.

"Fine. If you don't want to talk, that's fine. Why do I even bother?"

Joel maintained his silence. He held his breath while her face morphed into a scowl. Instead of lashing out, she spun and stormed out through the door of his room, letting it slam shut behind her.

———

In the morning light, the dream still terrified Joel. He couldn't remember the end of it, or even the beginning, though in the middle he felt a demonic possession had taken place. Joel remembered being on a stage. Rather, pushing a giant apple onto a stage before a crowd he couldn't see, blinded by the lighting. The apple was wooden, taller than he, and as round as he stood tall. No sooner had he shoved the monstrosity to the center of the stage than it opened, revealing a woman breastfeeding a small child. He knew the child then was a demon, and the woman was unaware. Joel tried to convince her to let the child go, and every time he failed, the crowd erupted in judgmental riotous laughter, until he finally admitted to himself that even as a child, the demon was stronger than he was. The echoes of the crowd's laughter followed him into wakefulness.

And so did thoughts of Lonnie.

Joel mulled over Lonnie and compared him to the actors in the dream. If Joel was himself, then perhaps Lonnie was the child and his mother was the scantily clad woman surrounded by the shell of an apple. By his mother's reaction every time Joel mentioned the man's name, he couldn't believe this to be the case. He struggled with the pieces until he gave up, unwilling to commit the role to anyone he actually knew.

Lonnie talks to the Lord.

Joel knew he did, because he'd seen him. The man never talked for very long without wishing a blessing on someone or proclaiming his faith. But in the Bible, in the top ten of the commandments that the Lord gave, was the one proclamation about killing. Then Joel thought of Sodom and Gomorrah, and pillars of salt. The Lord despised child molesters, he guessed, and probably would have treated a city of them the same. If Franklin was a child molester, then perhaps, just maybe, the Lord was just a little more specific to Lonnie about what he wanted than he was to most people.

And if Joel was honest with himself, hadn't he felt a spark of excitement at the man tied to the table? In the very least he hadn't done anything to stop it, and he thought he could have. If he'd told Lonnie not to do it, Joel believed that probably, Lonnie would have stopped.

Until he'd left. Then Lonnie would probably have killed the man anyway.

There was another option though.

Perhaps what he thought had happened was really just part of a dream. Maybe if he could remember the first part of his dream, it would connect what he thought was a memory from the previous evening to a dream sequence.

Grabbing on to this thought, Joel sprang up from bed and left his room, looking for a sign that anything was different. The hallways were just as bare, and when he emerged into the garden, the sun was just as bright as the day before. Following the cement path, he saw no footprints or anything that looked out of place. Emboldened, he made his way to the shed, which no longer bore the lock that he'd seen before, or any lock. He paused for a few seconds outside of the shed, working hard to convince himself that the evening was a dream. Then he screwed up his courage and pushed on the door hard enough for it to swing open and crash into the wall.

There was no table in the center of the gardening shed. Nothing indicated that anything untoward had occurred at all the evening before. It was only an empty shed. The entire evening must have been a dream.

"You're back." Lonnie's voice rose from behind him and shattered his hard-earned illusion. Joel turned in one smooth motion. Lonnie wore the same clothes from the previous night, and had a grin on his face that reached both ears. He carried no remorse and suffered nothing at all from his actions. Joel felt the envy well up inside of him. A *murderer* could feel the Lord, and he who had always done everything he was asked, felt nothing. Jealousy raged in his heart, and he stared deep into Lonnies green eyes.

"Can you teach me to feel the Lord?"

Lonnie's mouth spread open into a wide, snaggletoothed grin.

CHAPTER 11

AS JOEL AWAITED his first meeting with Lonnie in the tiny garden shed where Franklin, the child molester, had given up his life to the Lord, Joel felt stronger. His mother's frequent criticisms fell from his back, harmless darts against his protective turtle shell coating. Even in church, the absence of the Lord in his own heart only served to remind him that soon, soon he would be like Lonnie, so full of the Lord that he couldn't be contained to a single seat in the auditorium. Joel would transcend, and become one with the Lord.

When the day arrived, nearly a week later, the garden shed still only looked like a garden shed. Lonnie, on the other hand, looked more like a madman than he ever had before. The Lord works in mysterious ways.

"Welcome back, Mr. Joel," Lonnie told him as Joel stepped from the stifling heat of the outside into the even more stifling heat of the cramped shed. Joel nodded at him, though anxiety now welled inside his body and pinned his arms to his side while trapping his words in his throat.

"You asked me how I feel the Lord, and I offered to teach you."

"Y-yes..."

"What I need to know is whether you can stay committed to the course, Mr. Joel. Can you do everything the Lord asks of you?"

"I'm here, aren't I?"

"Answer the question though, Joel. Will you do whatever it takes? You saw what had to be done to that abomination. Can you do that, if the Lord wills it?"

Joel didn't hesitate.

"If the Lord wills it."

"That's good, Joel, good. Now ask me anything. What do you want to know?"

Joel felt his finger twitch as his heart ramped up. He fought the urge to leave. A voice in his mind told him that he'd given enough. But the desire was too strong, and he was too close to stop now.

"How do you feel the Lord?"

"I serve a purpose for the Lord, Joel. I purge the paeans. Those little people who won't commit to the Lord, or models who can't, these all meet justice at my hand."

"Justice meaning..."

"I think you know. But that's not all. Sometimes, every once in a while, the Lord asks for mercy for one of His own. And well, I do that too. Like Caitlyn Parker. The lady had offered so much faith up to the Lord, it was only fitting that He ask me to be merciful to her, and bring her to a peaceful death."

"*You* killed her?"

"The Lord killed her, Mr. Joel. I am only his instrument."

Joel's head grew hot and he struggled to keep it upright

as the room slowly tilted before him. Willpower alone kept him on his feet. This woman trusted his mother and donated her entire savings to the church in lieu of medical treatment. Her reward, or the Lord's reward, was death.

"She didn't do anything to anyone."

Lonnie shook his head slowly to the right and the left, his eyes glassy.

"The road before her was a hard one. The cancer, a tool of the devil, spread and she was in pain every hour of every day. The Lord asked me to call her to Him."

The man's eyes suddenly seemed sunken into his face, as though he had never slept in his life. His furrowed eyebrows portrayed a deep and profound sadness, a sadness that surprised Joel by reflecting in himself, deep down beneath the layers of his own self-loathing. He felt something spark and held his breath, afraid to snuff the ember before it lit.

"A good woman."

Lonnie nodded.

"It was hard to do that one, but the Lord..."

"The Lord demanded it. You said. Did you use that blue stuff?"

"No," Lonnie said without embellishment.

"How many people have you killed?"

"Has the Lord killed, you mean? I don't know, I lost count. Maybe thirty, I guess."

Joel thought back to the disappearances in the church, and he shuddered. There had been at least that many, if not twice that in the last year alone. But his conviction wouldn't fail him. He re-committed himself. A single life is nothing compared to the Lord.

"Who's next?"

Lonnie smiled a weak, gentle grin. "I thought you'd never

ask." With that he produced a tablet from beneath the garden tools, dropped haphazardly into a box as though it were another pair of sheers. Lonnie flicked his finger across the screen, and a face appeared of a woman, older with thick graying hair and eyes that had almost no pupils in them.

"This one, she's a non-believer. She comes in every weekend, takes notes down, and reports them to her disgusting virtual reality show. She mocks the church and in doing so, mocks the Lord."

"I've never seen her before." Joel was certain of that, at least among the limited in-person members. She could have been a virtual member, but those were anywhere in the world, and Joel somehow didn't believe that Lonnie traveled worldwide to carry out his missions.

"You wouldn't, Mr. Joel," Lonnie told him. "She's too crafty for that, as are all the evil ones. Her disguises are many."

"How does she get on the list week after week? Can't we just kick her out?"

"She changes her name every time, and her look. I didn't see her until she left last time, dressed like a man in a dim green jacket." Lonnie spat the words, and Joel could tell that Lonnie already felt something about the woman, something he would no doubt understand to be the Lord. Joel felt nothing.

"How do we do it?"

"I do it. But she's useful, so we will use her. If you want to understand how to deliver paeans to the Lord, it begins with invisibility."

"Paeans?"

"Like the psalms. Each one is a tribute to the Lord, a song in its own right. These people are the way people like us worship Him. The most important rule is that we can't be seen."

Joel had felt invisible for his entire life, so he felt like this was something that was designed for him to be successful at. He smiled automatically, and Lonnie caught his smile.

"Oh, it's easy, eh? We'll see about that, I suppose. For now, close your eyes and think of the Lord."

Joel did as he was asked.

"Now, visualize it. You're walking down poplar street, and you see God's chosen target. You cross the street to where she stands, and walk just behind her, close enough for her to hear your footsteps. She walks faster, and you think she might know you're there. Faster still, and finally she breaks out into a dead run, but you're faster. You catch her quickly, and then bring her here. How do you get her here?"

"Trunk of a vehicle. It would be simple."

"Someone might see you."

"Not if I walk slowly, just stay close enough for her not to see me, until she ducks into an alley or something. Then put her in."

"What vehicle? If you want her back here, you have to get her to go where you want her to go. Your vehicle has to be there already, waiting for you and ready to go."

"I see."

The point of the impromptu lesson landed well: kidnapping was a lot more work than he probably thought. Hours upon hours of tracking and note-taking had to be involved. They had to know about every aspect of the paean's life, from morning through evening. They had to know the schedules of the people in the person's life too.

"You don't yet, but you will," Lonnie said. "Today, we gather intel."

Fifteen minutes later, sunlight penetrated the translucent membrane of the volantrae as they lifted off just beyond church grounds. The flying transport was a Falcon, and the newest model, shaped like the bird it emulated, complete down to the outspread highly-ornamental wings and talons beneath. Joel stepped up through a door that swung down from the bird's chest to take his place on the couch-like passenger seat, isolated from the pilot's chair suspended overhead in the bird's neck. That he left for Lonnie.

"This is nice," Joel said, touching the faux-leather seat by his leg with the tips of his fingers.

"The Lord provides," was all Lonnie said in response.

The meticulous way that Lonnie obeyed the traffic laws seemed overkill, especially considering the man could have let the hover drive itself.

"Why don't you just let it self-navigate?"

"And advertise where we're going to whoever happens to be watching, Mr. Joel? No."

A bus cut over above them close enough that Joel could make out the thrusters beneath it and the way the flames flared out against the top of the Falcon.

"Do you have to fly so close?"

"Mr. Joel, you are here to learn, and I'm here to teach."

Another way of saying to stop asking questions. This relationship between them seemed to be one-way. Joel's job was to listen and obey, a skill that he'd polished through years of life with his mother. His stomach lifted as Joel felt the volantrae descend, and he looked up to see League City spread out before him. They landed on Strata 1, the first layer above ground-level.

"Let's go."

"You know where she is?"

"I told you, the Lord will provide."

Joel followed Lonnie from the vehicle, stepping onto the elevated sidewalk. One level beneath them, he could see cars pulling out from alleyways, cluttering intersections, as a pedestrian and bus nearly collided. On their level, the sidewalks were elevated and made of something that resembled composite rubber. What as informally called the Canopy connected multiple levels of buildings across the city, spanning out like spider webs from each building. Volantrae of different shapes passed between and over the different Strata. There was never an intersection of traffic and civilians outside of the buildings.

As Joel struggled to catch up to Lonnie's impatient march, he paid more attention to buildings in the vicinity of the convoluted walkway network. One nearby building was a bank, which towered into the upper levels of the city. Of two others in close proximity, one was a community plaza, which only extended from the looks of it up to the third level over their heads. The last was a municipal library, nearly as tall as the bank, but much fatter, resembling a stout fighter, crouched and ready to trade blows.

"In there." Lonnie pointed through the glass as they approached the community plaza, closed off by tall glass doors from the interior. At a counter, seated on a stool, sipping something that may have been coffee or cocoa — or yaupon tea, a delicacy in South Texas — sat the woman in the image that Lonnie had shown Joel earlier.

"The Lord provides," Lonnie whispered again, clearly oblivious to the fact that Joel wasn't buying into this part of his spiel at all. It was all too convenient. Lonnie had known that the woman would be there, of course, and this meant that he'd been stalking the woman for how long? Joel didn't want to think about it. A gust of wind blew past them with a hollow whispering sound.

"Coming?"

"I don't understand. She has a holovision show and speaks out against our church. So what? Lots of people do that, and have for decades. We can't kill them all."

"Mr. Joel, come through the door so we stop making a scene. Remember, we need to stay invisible."

Joel acquiesced and traversed the door finally, letting it slam shut behind him. The woman glanced up quickly and then went back to sipping her beverage.

"What's the real reason?"

"Look with your heart, Joel. What do you see?"

Joel examined the woman more closely, tilting his head slightly as he did so. She casually brushed a wayward strand of hair back from her face and bit her lower lip while she focused on the tablet before her. He'd seen that mannerism before. He recognized her from somewhere, but couldn't place it. Only a handful of years older than him, maybe ten at the most, he could almost place her. The hair fell back before her face and she blew at it, cementing the image in his mind.

"Carol?"

"See, Mr. Joel, I knew you would see."

Carol Barbary used to belong to the church, and occasionally babysat for Joel when he was younger. Back then, when his parents had been together, they'd been allowed use of the holovid for children's shows when his parents were away at their adult entertainment in the city. He remembered her vividly now, sitting on the couch and ignoring his episodes of Adventures of Plim, about an android who had to be taught every single facet of human emotion. But now that he placed her, the idea of her death made even less sense.

The Lord wouldn't care about her. Or if He did, He would want to bring her back, surely, not dead.

"Her words, they poison the people. The whore of Babylon speaks and turns hearts away from the Lord, so that He wants her silenced."

"She's not a whore of Babylon. She's just Carol."

"With a million acolytes," Lonnie said, nodding in her direction just as a younger woman approached where Carol sat. Joel watched the scene before him as the younger woman leaned in, examined Carol's face, and then stepped back and put her hands over her mouth.

"Oh my god! It's you! I want to thank you so much, you got my brother out of that place."

That place, Joel knew, had to be Austin Life Community Church. Carol put down her tablet and smiled at the woman.

"Thank God for that. Some people never get out. You are?"

"Jenny," said the young woman. "You can call me Jenny. Can you sign... uh..."

"Here," Carol said, and reached into a bag on the seat beside her. She produced a book and a pen, and lay the book on the desk, then scribbled with a pen on the inside cover.

"Jenny, your brother will need years of therapy to get past what's happened to him."

She slid the book across the table and Jenny picked it up. Joel noticed Jenny's smile fade, and then she nodded.

"He's already started. It's not easy."

"It won't be. There will be days that he's convinced that you are against him, and that the church is all there is. Those will be the hardest, but they will pass. They did for me."

Joel stood quickly, and began to cross the chasm of floor tiles between them. Lonnie grabbed at Joel's arm, and missed as Joel shrugged him off. Carol betrayed his mother, and her church, and her Lord. The Lord's righteous fury channeled through him, and he stopped cold in realization of that fact. For the first time, perhaps ever, he felt the Lord, and it was wrath that the Lord unleashed in him. Then he continued his forward momentum, closing the distance to her table. Carol looked up at him, her eyes void of recognition as the woman named Jenny left. Then Carol's eyes went wide as they met his, and now Joel knew that she recognized him.

"Officer," she called, and a man who Joel hadn't noticed turned in his periphery. "Isn't it a beautiful day?"

Her words were for the policeman that Joel had missed, but she never broke her eyes away from Joel's face.

"Why?" He asked the question as he arrived a the table. "Why would you do something like that to us?"

The policeman made his way to the table where Carol sat.

"Hey Carol," he said to her.

"Oh, I didn't know it was you Min-Lau. Care to join?"

The officer's eyes went from Carol's face to Joel's then back.

"Maybe I will."

He pulled up a seat.

"What's your name, son?"

"Joel Emerson Haines," Carol answered for him, still not breaking eye contact. The officer's eyes now fixated on Joel, narrowing his gaze as he scrutinized Joel's features.

"Haines?" Something about the way the man said his name told him that the officer knew of the church, and didn't approve.

"We were just leaving, Officer," Joel heard Lonnie's voice chime out behind him.

"Good idea," the officer responded.

———

Lonnie wasn't his usual chipper self on the ride back to the church complex. He set the volantrae on auto-pilot, leaned back and closed his eyes. Joel watched him as his own heart pummeled itself into the sides of his rib cage like a ping-pong ball. Joel felt waves of disappointment, one after another, crash into his chest. Sometimes his heart hit the front of his chest from one side when a wave of malaise hit on the other, and he could feel the forces do brief battle in a flutter of energy. Then, nothing as they both dissolved into silence.

"I didn't mean to, he said, because he had to say something in the void.

"Maybe you aren't ready for the Lord's work."

The words, produced with a kind tone, even a slightly appreciatory one, drilled into Joel's ears.

"I'm ready."

"Not if you can't control yourself, you're not."

"I didn't know..."

Two green eyes shot open and Lonnie's head pivoted toward Joel.

"I told you what we were there to do, and who it was we were watching. You decided to ignore all of that and go up to the woman. You know what that means, right?"

"Try again, but do better?"

"No. That means we can't touch her now. There was a policeman there, and that policeman now knows who you are, and who I am. The paean knows who you are, and right now she's telling all her friends. What happens when she disappears?"

Joel buried his head in his hands and didn't answer. Instead, he felt deep down, looking for the Lord to guide him, but again, the Lord wasn't there. All that occupied his shell of a body was Lonnie's disillusionment, and it overflowed through his eyes as they collected his grievances in the form of tears that Joel refused to let fall.

"Give me another chance?"

Lonnie's entire body heaved as he sighed and sank back into his chair.

"To mess it up again?"

"To do it right."

"Mr. Joel, I don't know if you can do this."

"Train me then. I'll learn."

The man pushed a thick hand through red hair, and smiled with just the corners of his mouth.

"I guess, Mr. Joel. Maybe I got it wrong. Maybe the killing's the first thing you got to learn, and the tracking's the next thing. Maybe that's the order."

CHAPTER 12

THE IDEA of taking another life percolated itself into a dream. In this nightmare, Joel stood armed with a proton rifle, a gun with a short stocky grip and a long barrel that made him look like he held a rake by the pointy end. He guarded a group of people who were trapped inside a loose barbed-wire fence. The absolute certainty only available in dreams told him that he needed to kill the one that the Lord told him to. But since he couldn't actually hear the Lord, they all looked the same, and they all stared up at him with pleading, dark eyes as a voice echoed out behind him.

"The Lord demands it, Mr. Joel."

Only it didn't sound like the airy, ambivalent voice of Lonnie. That voice was deeper and multi-tonal, a cross between his father's voice, and his mother's, and Lonnie's. One small voice chimed out beside him.

"You don't have to decide, Joel. This isn't the Lord's work."

He awoke with Delilah's words echoing through his head. He didn't have to choose, and it wasn't the Lord's work.

Shaken, Joel tried a quick shower to reset his mind, but it didn't help. He slowly made his way through the clutter in his room and out into the main part of the house.

"Are you okay Joel?"

He jerked his head up to the left, to meet his mother's scrutinizing gaze. She always asked the same question, and he always gave the same answer. He wondered why they even bothered the routine.

"Yes, I'm fine," he confirmed, nodding his head to drive the point home. Her narrowing gaze conveyed that she didn't believe him, but she didn't press.

"It's a big day today, Joel. I'm nervous too, but the key is not to show it. Gather yourself together."

"Big day?"

She reached for a coffee cup before her, and slowly took a sip, without breaking eye contact.

"You don't remember?"

"No."

"Franklin Thomas' funeral."

"The child molester? We have to go to that?"

"Alleged, Joel. And they've asked me to officiate, so yes, we have to go."

"Do I have to?"

Joel's mother still stared. She'd been expecting his response, he guessed. Her unblinking stare was all the answer she would give. It would be all the answer that she would need to give. That was the level of control she had over him, and he was always powerless against her. Then she broke eye contact, her eyes darting towards the door, and he followed suit.

"Came for you today. I found it outside but didn't open it. Did you get some new tools?"

Joel's eyes fell then on a light-beige box fastened with a golden clip that looked something like a belt. He scanned it over for a note, but none was attached. Lonnie had decided that Joel needed to start killing, but would the man be so brash to deliver murder supplies through his mother? It was the same size as his engineering kit that he used to work on the VR servers. He couldn't remember having ordered a new kit though.

"Thanks, Mom."

Joel grabbed it by the handle on the top and hefted it up into the air.

"Are you going to open it?"

The last thing he wanted to do was open it if his mother hovered nearby.

"A new VR toolkit, that's all. No, I'll just put it away."

He spirited the box back to his room, and placed it on his bed. Then he stared at it, curious of its contents, but still hearing dream Delilah's voice telling him he was making a mistake. Taking a deep breath, he unlatched it and examined the contents.

The first thing that he saw before him was a thick role of ventilation tape, wide and purple. Next to that were three knives, each a slightly different shape and length. One had a curve from the short metal handle, looking like a miniature scythe. Another thinned quickly and came to a point, and the last was a short, stubby thing in a small holster. He closed the lid and shuddered again without looking further.

A knock on his door made him jump up to his feet. He looked around for a place to hide the box, but found nowhere to put it. He latched it back with the golden buckle, and then walked toward the door to answer it.

"Mr. Joel, are you in?"

"Coming."

Joel shuffled to the door and then popped it open, to see Lonnie's smiling and expectant face looming in the doorway.

"I guess you should come in," he said to the man, who didn't wait for him to finish the invitation before pushing his way into the room. Joel made a quick check for his mother before he latched the door behind Lonnie.

"I told you it was time. We're going to try it differently this time. We're going to try to train you here so you can't mess it up. Here being on the complex," Lonnie explained.

"You think I'm ready?"

"It's not like you have to do anything. I'll go track them down — bring them here and then I can show you how to do it. Not much to it."

Joe looked at Lonnie's deep-set eyes. Those green eyes fixed on him and seemed to judge his every response to see if he would measure up to doing the Lord's work.

"Okay," Joel said, pushing down the queasiness in his stomach. "You already have somebody here?"

"No. Takes time to do these things. You botched the last one so we need to find the next."

"Well, who's next on the list?"

"In time. Right now. Let's take a look at what I got you."

With that, Lonnie approached the box like a new toy that a he'd just gotten for Christmas. Popping open the lid, he pulled out the first thing that Joel had seen earlier; the tape.

"Once you get your paean, you definitely don't want them to escape. That's what this is for. Strapped down tight and taped up, they're not going anywhere. Unless you set them free."

"Do you ever set them free?"

The man shook his red mane.

"That doesn't happen. But still it's up to the Lord, isn't it?"

Lonnie moved on to the next item, and pulled out the three knives.

"Sometimes, the Lord wants them to be taught a lesson first. When that happens, you need to be ready to oblige."

Joel's stomach turned as he internalized the message that torture was part of the Lord's work. Lonnie put the knives down and reach back to pick up something else.

"Your communicator. So we can get in touch without having to worry about being detected. Encrypted and everything. Doesn't ring and doesn't buzz very loudly, but you need to keep it on you just in case. When the Lord wants things done, He wants things done right away."

He handed the communicator over to Joel, who shoved it into his pocket. The Lord probably didn't need a communicator, he considered. They looked through the rest of the box's contents, but by that point the room had begun to spin and Joel's head began to throb. The only other items he noticed were three little vials of powder next to a tube of some sort of liquid paste — the tools to create Lonnie's death concoction.

Then Joel sat on the bed, listening to Lonnie's voice fade into and out of the background noises. He heard, layered over the excited intonations, Delilah's voice from the dream.

"Not the Lord's way."

CHAPTER 13

BY THE TIME Church came around again on the next Saturday morning, Joel had gotten used to having the toolbox under his bed. He'd warmed to it even, and in the evenings, he pulled out the blades and turned them over in his hands, admiring the sharp honed edges and the way they felt in his palms. He tossed them and practice flipping them around, although he knew such a skill as knife-flipping was of no practical use. As he left for his pre-sermon equipment check, he packed them away back into the kit and slid it under his bed, carefully hidden deep in the back against the wall so no one would find it who didn't already know it was there.

On his way to the main church building, Joel noticed electricity in the air around him. He took that to be a sign that he had finally discovered the right path. Despite his misgivings and confusion, he finally made his way toward the Lord. Others seem to notice too, chief among these being his mother, whose presence he'd just left.

"Joel, honey, did you check the virtual reality equipment?"

He'd scowled at her for reminding him. Every weekend, it was the same routine, and he'd never forgotten. The difference was in how she responded.

"I-I'm sorry, Joel. I know you can do it, and you always do. I just get nervous still, that's all."

His mother never apologized for anything, to anyone. Yet just that morning, she had given him an unsolicited apology, and instead of her usual cryptic disapproval, she'd offered compassion and acquiescence.

Joel breezed through the morning and past the usual sermon, sneaking a grin toward Lonnie as he gyrated in the crowd, full of life and channeling the Lord. Lightness followed wherever Joel went, and to his surprise, the feeling lasted past the sermon and into Bible study, where Delilah had saved him a seat. She seemed to have forgiven him for his denial of her. As he took his place in the circle, he couldn't help noticing that her gaze had fixated on him, and her eyes seemed to ferret over his body, looking for something that he couldn't imagine.

Something else about her seemed off. She seemed thinner, and when she talked, her cheeks seemed to stretch to the point of almost breaking. Her neck seemed to have to work constantly to keep head upright, stretching tendons there taught. As the circle leader guided the discussion with his usual prods and accusations, her eyes darted back to Joel at erratic intervals.

His confidence held all the way through Bible study. He even returned her stare twice, keeping it as long as she did until she seemed to realize she did it, and looked away again. But she kept doing it, and as she did, he felt his confidence drip away with every glance. Eventually irritation seeped into him, replacing the feeling altogether. Then he heard the circle leader interrupt.

"Well, we've been going for an hour straight now. Does anyone need a break before we get more into Luke?"

Joel's hand was the first up, but it wasn't the only one.

"Fifteen minutes," the circle leaders said. "Fifteen minutes and then right back here. We have a lot to get through still."

Then Joel made his way to the hallway, where Delilah found him.

"You seem different," she commented, as his heart raced in his chest.

"What do you mean?"

"I mean, something about you. You seem better somehow. Did something change?" Then she lowered her voice into a whisper. "Are you on medication?"

When she asked the question, however irritated Joel was then, he knew that it was out of concern, instead of analytical curiosity or condemnation. Or at least he believed it to be so.

"No, nothing's changed."

"Well, *something's* changed. You don't look like somebody punched your puppy anymore. You're better."

Joel glared at the puppy-punching reference, then shifted his weight from one leg to the other, and turned his body so that he was not directly facing her, hoping that the change in posture would be enough to dissuade Delilah from further questions. But Delilah was type of person who would nibble around the edges until she got to the truth — and the truth he wasn't ready to share yet. Even if he had been, he couldn't imagine that Delilah would understand.

She glared right back.

"Why are you staring like that?" He asked.

"What are you trying to hide?"

"I'm not trying to hide anything. It's just Bible study."

And just then, to Joel's perceived salvation, the circle leader's voice rang out behind them.

"One minute, One minute, everyone."

Her features slackened and her eagle-stare wavered.

"Do you want to skip?"

Joel nodded before realizing what he was doing, remembering the days before when they spent hours in the garden together.

"Let's do it. I already know everything there is to know about the book of Luke."

Joel laughed, because he was certain she did. She'd been attending the church as long as he had, and she was smarter than him. By now, the entire Bible was nestled away behind those green eyes and freckles.

"Me too."

As they walked past the open door and straight through the building, Joel felt his confidence returning. His heart skipped when the backs of her fingers brushed against his. In silence, they emerged into the sunlit morning, and he felt the tips of her fingers work their way through his, then grip his hand tightly. Confused, Joel took a moment to look at her, taking in the profile of her face against the backdrop of nature, and he noticed something he'd missed before. In her look lurked a subdued loss. He had changed, but something about her, and the fierce grip she now clutched his hand with, told him that maybe she had too.

For the first few minutes, the pair walked in silence together, listening to the birds that frequented the branches of the poplar and pecan trees, and the yaupon clusters. They took a different route this time, and instead of moving toward their old bench just to the east of the main building, where they'd so frequently been interrupted by Lonnie, they moved toward the south. Joel allowed Delilah to lead down the cement paths, as he'd seen everything so often that one spot was as good as the next, as long as she maintained that grip on his now-sweaty hands. She brought them to a stop before a giant oak.

"It's been here for a century," she said, her voice quivering as she stared up at it. The comment pulled his eyes toward it. "Survived climate change and everything, and kept pushing up toward the sky."

His eyes followed the curve of the gnarled trunk upwards and to the wide branches that loomed overhead and blotted out the sun. The Spanish moss hung in sheets from it, clinging to the mighty protector. The archangel Raphael sprang into his mind, holding the moss like a shield before him, pushing back the forces of evil.

"That's older than the church."

She nodded. "The church used to meet under it, my mom says. Back when there were only a handful of them. Your parents, my parents, a few others — people looking for a better way to celebrate the Lord. They were going to build the church around the tree, actually — but they didn't want to kill it."

Joel smiled at the idea of his father and mother, and Delilah's parents, gathered together under the oak's protective branches, reading from the Bible. In his mental image, they smiled, and laughed, and praised the Lord. There was no virtual reality equipment to maintain, no donations to keep up with, or bills to pay even. A group of worshipers together, with no other agenda to speak of.

"Joel, I wanted to tell you before it starts circulating."

He directed his attention toward her, focused initially on her face. But she used her hands when she spoke, and his eyes latched onto her wrists, which he now noticed had shrunken to the point of non-existence. Delilah swallowed, and choked back a cough.

"I'm dying, Joel. It's just a matter of time, really. We found out last week, but I couldn't tell you then — you didn't seem strong enough."

"You're not dying," he denied, dropping his eyes from hers and staring at the ground.

"It won't help to deny it."

"How can you be dying? The Lord wouldn't want that. The Lord..."

"Works in his own ways, Joel. When it's time, it's time. We don't really get a choice in the matter, do we?"

He opened his mouth to protest more, but she drew her lips to his and kissed him instead. The kiss drew him into her, lingering, ponderous and gentle. They stood, breathing each other in, long after their lips parted. Joel pulled his arms around her, gazing into her eyes, mind spiking out like a porcupine as he explored alternative ways to save her, even though he knew nothing about her illness yet.

"Cancer," she told him in barely a whisper. "Already metastasized. Do you know what that means?"

Joel had seen enough death to speak its language.

"Everywhere," he replied, clutching tightly.

"Everywhere," she nodded. He could see then the tears that had formed in her eyes, and recognized the effort she made to keep him calm. A feeling emerged inside of him, something deep and fearful, hiding behind the feeling that he'd once thought to be the Lord. He really was Job, and this was his test. Delilah would be taken from him.

The thought enraged him as he felt his heart quicken and pulled away. These games that the Lord played, pushing her into his life only to yank her away again. Asking impossible things of him, like murdering on His behalf, and then Joel's reward being only for the Lord to murder the woman he loved. He knew his eyes had furrowed up into tents of hostility, and he pulled away fast, turning so she couldn't see the pain twist his features.

"Joel, it will be okay," she lied.

"You know it won't," he replied to her through gritted teeth. "What does it matter anyway, any of this. We twist and struggle and try to understand, and at the end, it's all stolen from us."

But maybe there was a way. The idea emerged into his mind fully formed. Maybe this wasn't the test that he thought it was, but perhaps it was the Lord making sure that he kept his promise to Lonnie. All he had to do was follow instructions, kill whoever the Lord needed killed, and then Delilah would be cured. But right now, the Lord saw her as a distraction, and something that needed to be dealt with.

"I have to go," he told her without looking at her, and finally pulled his fingers from hers. Then he turned away as she tried to keep his grip, ignoring the tiny whimper that she let out.

"Joel, wait. What's going on? Where are you going?"

He ignored her and swallowed down the guilt and the pain. If the Lord wanted loyalty and obedience, he was well-practiced at it. He stumbled away from Delilah as his body resisted his intention, asserting that he made the wrong decision, and that really, he needed to stay with her under the tree. But he couldn't listen. Every moment she remained a distraction, she died a little more. The Lord wanted what the

Lord wanted, and Joel couldn't stand in His way. Joel made his way back to the eastern part of the garden. There, the little shed waited before him, ominous in the way the light seemed to bounce off of it, denied entrance and expelled back into the world. He took a few cautious steps toward it, and then pushed his way through the door. There, on a stool sharpening one of his knives, sat Lonnie.

"I knew you'd come here soon, Mr. Joel."

CHAPTER 14

JOEL HADN'T EXPECTED Lonnie to do much with regards to training, since he seemed to be yanked back and forth by the fluid will of the Lord, which sometimes manifested in raging rants, and other times devolved into explosions of tears. Despite the chaotic nature of their time together, Joel began to discern a pattern. For one thing, Lonnie rarely had outbursts once training began. A session might be pre-empted by Lonnie expounding loudly on some external event, whatever the latest news headlines were. Inevitably once he'd exhausted the topic, Lonnie became calm and was clear about his expectations of what Joel needed to learn for the day.

Days turned into weeks that turned into over a month, all the time avoiding Delilah and skipping Bible study altogether to further his real training. To him, the Bible had transfigured into a useful historical reference, while training was about the next chapter in the Lord's journey. Joel even fantasized about writing a book one day, something that might be added to canon, about his experiences.

But first, he had to prove that he could do the Lord's work. And late on a Friday, Lonnie had a surprise for him.

"Today, Joel," he said, while tossing Joel the keys to the volantrae that he owned. The gesture was a symbolic one, Joel recognized, as symbols were another level of communication Lonnie used regularly. Joel was in charge for the day, and finally, he would be allowed to track his own paean. Attempting not to betray his excitement, and considering what this might mean for Delilah's health, Joel kept an even tone.

"Who's the paean today?"

"This man."

Lonnie retrieved his pinamu from the bucket below, and Joel recognized the face as a one-time parishioner of the church.

"What'd he do?"

"The Lord has said that he's lost his way. He has transitioned to atheism, and like the others, he speaks out against the church, and so against the Lord."

"Another one?"

"There've been a lot lately, Mr. Joel. It happens this way sometimes — in spells it seems. If we do the Lord's work properly, it will stop."

"Amen."

"Amen to that, Mr. Joel. It's not all doom and gloom, though. Sometimes, and these are the ones I like — sometimes the Lord calls in people early. Sometimes their suffering on this planet is done, and it's just time and somehow they didn't realize it yet. Those, Mr. Joel, are the most beautiful. Then you can see when they give up their spirits to the Lord. You can just about see them rise up to heaven."

For a second, Joel imagined what that must be like, spirit rising from a body, smiling and loving and aglow in the Lord's light.

"Are you ready?"

Joel nodded.

"Let's go."

This time, they started at the paean's home. Since the paean had been a member of the church, it was simple to find out where he lived, and simpler still to park across the street from his townhouse in the late afternoon and watch as the burly, bearded paean pulled in to park and left his car. Joel watched the paean exit through the car door — it was a car, not one of the oddly-shaped volantrae that soared overhead. Joel made a note of that since it limited the likelihood of places he could travel as they wouldn't have to chase him around in the upper levels. The Austin canopy of higher-level skybridges, small by most standards as the residents had placed limits on expansion, was still a confusing mesh to work through with its one-way lanes.

"What now, Mr. Joel?"

The question was a prompt, or an indication that he'd forgotten something. Joel thought through the process as he'd been taught. Start at the person's home, as that's the base of operations, and the paean would always return. Mark their transportation somehow to make it easier to track. That was next.

Joel reached across into the seat beside him to retrieve a dark orange permanent marker. Then, keeping low as he crossed the street, he circled around to each tire, making a bold orange mark near the bottom. It was the same color that traffic police often used to mark parking violations, so even if the marks were noticed, nobody would think twice this close to the city. He glanced quickly up at the townhouse and saw movement in one of the windows, then froze. Sliding the marker into his pocket, he stood, only daring to re-check the window once he was on his feet. The shadow he'd noticed before was gone. Joel made his way back to the car.

"Good, next time check more. Look over there."

Across from them, a woman stood, examining a "For Sale" sign on a home across the street, and Joel mentally kicked himself. He'd been so focused on whether the paean had seen him that he hadn't taken in his surroundings.

"That's okay, Mr. Joel. You should have seen me on my first time. It was a mess."

Joel, checking to make sure the door to the volantrae had shut properly after he entered, looked at Joel.

"First time?"

Since he found out about Joel's work for the Lord, Joel had never asked about his first time, nor had Lonnie offered any information on how he'd gotten into the Lord's business.

"Well, I didn't know it was the Lord's work at first. Neither did my parents. They thought there was something wrong with me, honestly, Mr. Joel. But you see, I had to practice for the Lord, you know? And sometimes I felt bad about it."

Joel hadn't ever seen anything that he thought looked like regret coming from Lonnie before. There'd been anger and sadness, and even overwhelming joy, but not regret.

"I can still see those little birds, and their crippled little wings. But now I know — it was practice. The Lord needed me to be ready, and so he made it so that I couldn't stop."

"Couldn't stop what?"

The story had changed. Joel now realized that he wasn't

going to hear about Lonnie's first time, but he remained curious just the same.

"He would bring them to me, you know? Land them right there on my windowsill, and they'd come to my hands. Once they got there, my hands did their work."

Joel saw Lonnie bring up his hands together and then make a quick twisting motion, snapping an imaginary bird's neck, or breaking a wing, tearing a leg perhaps. What the gesture meant was evasive, but explicit at the same time.

Lonnie had always enjoyed killing.

Joel caught movement from the corner of his eye.

"He's moving," he said, shaking off the disturbing feeling that came with his new knowledge.

"We move too then, Mr. Joel."

They pulled away from the curb at the same time as the tiny car did, and fell into pace behind their mark.

After following the paean for an entire day, and recording his habits, Joel began to feel comfortable in his assignment. He stayed far enough back not to be seen, and switched to skyways where it made sense to stay out of sight, yet keep the tiny car visible. Overall, even Lonnie had to say at the end of the day that he'd done what he'd been asked to do.

"Well done, Mr. Joel. Got your notes?"

Joel nodded briskly.

"Let's go home then. Enough for now. Do you feel ready?"

"For..."

"Tomorrow. Think of it as kind of a test. All you have to do is track this man again, see what he does again, and what he doesn't. Got to do that for about a week, and then we can make a plan."

"By myself?"

"You don't think you're ready."

Joel considered the statement, which came out as more of a question according to the inquisitive look on Lonnie's face. This was it, wasn't it? Graduation of sorts to the next level, one step closer to doing the Lord's work, and Joel couldn't tell why he balked at it.

"I'm ready."

———

The next morning, Joel beat his mother to the kitchen for breakfast and skipped out just as she entered. He'd skillfully managed to avoid her, which meant that she was preoccupied with some cataclysmic problem or another, since she hadn't demanded the truth of what he did with all of his time now that working with Lonnie had taken the place of his Bible study classes. Joel had a lie ready just in case, but he hope not to use it as he didn't need to add to his debt to the Lord.

Lonnie fussed over him like a parent sending a child off, made him check everything twice.

"I'll be fine. I'll do the exact same thing as yesterday."

"Mr. Joel, don't go in thinking that. He may do everything completely different. You gotta stay focused, and be careful. Maybe this was a mistake."

"Lonnie, you're going to have to trust me sometime. How else will I be able to do the Lord's work if you don't let me learn?"

Lonnie didn't argue with that, but the concern never left his face.

"Half a day. That's good enough. Just through noon and

come back and let me know. Or call the communicator. Do you have your kit?"

Joel nodded. Lonnie had seen him put the kit in the back of the volantrae, so Joel didn't know why he still asked about it.

"There's one more thing, Mr. Joel."

"Stop worrying, Lonnie."

"Just, be careful okay? I've never worked with anybody on the Lord's work before. I don't — don't want to lose you yet."

"What are you talking about?"

Even as he asked the question he noticed the glossiness in Lonnie's eyes. The man barely held back tears, he realized. Joel lowered his voice.

"I'll be fine."

An awkward goodbye later, and Joel was on his way, straight to the man's home. When he pulled off of the church grounds, his hands began to shake involuntarily on the steering controls.

"Engage autopilot," he told the vehicle. "Same place as yesterday."

He pulled his hands away from he y-shaped steering controls and held them before his eyes, watching them vibrate and willing them to stop. His mind went through all of the ways that he could screw up his simple mission, back to that first foray into he city. Joel swallowed and closed his eyes, attempting to calm his nerves by clearing his mind, but then he caught sight of Delilah's face and his hands shook further. Would she understand the Lord's work that he'd agreed to? Joel didn't know, and that left him so anxious and afraid that he didn't notice when the volantrae came to a stop in front of the man's home, but on the wrong side of the street. He looked up to see the tiny car just before him, and immediately slouched down into his seat just in time to see the man push through his gate in the corner of Joel's eye.

Joel didn't find the courage to sit back up and look until he heard the tiny car pull away from the curb. Only then did he start the volantrae up again and follow, staying behind him as he'd been taught.

Unlike the previous day of driving around the city from stop to stop, this time the paean made one quick right turn, then a left and pulled back to the curb. Fear of losing him made Joel follow the pattern, though he knew that he should continue straight and try to find him by traveling in the same general direction. Joel waited against the curb, watching as the man exited his car and turned to face Joel directly. Then, in a half run, the man approached Joel's volantrae, and he knew that he'd been spotted. Still, Joel tried to become invisible by slouching in his seat again, but only surfaced when he heard the raps on the windowed dome covering the volantrae.

"Hey, what are you doing?" He heard the man yelling through the glass.

"Can you tell me how to get to fifth?" Joel responded with his own question, thin and weak, but plausible.

"Don't give me that. I know this is the same volantrae as yesterday. Where's your partner?"

"I don't know what you're talking about."

"Yes you do. Why are you following me? Are you the IRS?"

"No sir," came a familiar voice, and Joel craned his neck to see where the voice came from. "Securities and Exchange Commission."

Joel's stomach dropped as he saw Lonnie materialize

behind him in a trim suit and tie. He hadn't realized that Lonnie even had multiple volantrae. There seemed no end to the things he didn't now about the man.

"W-what are you following me for?"

"Let's start with insider trading, and where should we stop?"

The man's flustered face told Joel that Lonnie's words had landed. The small house on Strata 1, the tiny car, and the endless driving through the city in his worker's commute didn't add up to insider trading to Joel, but the man's guilty face implied the words were true.

"I didn't know, and I gave the money back."

"It's routine, sir. We need to know who you talk to, follow up on some things, that's all. Just pretend we aren't here. That's probably the best way to do it. We'll be out of your hair before you know it."

This seemed to convince the man, as he returned to his vehicle. Joel pushed the button to retract the dome covering.

"Time to go home, Mr. Joel. We'll have to try again later, I expect."

"I can still do it. You just told him..."

"I know what I told him. Right now, he's probably checking on me. Didn't even ask for my badge, did he? This paean's not stupid, and now he knows what we look like. Got to go, Mr. Joel."

His words didn't come out aggressive or angry sounding, but the way Lonnie's shoulders slumped slightly, and the way his eyes bounced around but wouldn't meet Joel's, conveyed all the message that he needed. Lonnie was disappointed.

Today was a test, and Joel had failed.

Joel beat Lonnie home, and took the opportunity to drop the keys into the shed and make his way back home with his kit, which he then hid back away in its hiding place beneath his bed. His mother was out doing church business somewhere, so he had the house to himself, a nice secluded spot to nurse his wounded ego. At the current rate, he'd never get to doing the Lord's work, a prospect that filled him with an odd mixture of fear and relief. He'd just settled himself into the couch when the house beeped at him, indicating that someone had approached the front door who wasn't on the automatic approve list.

His breathing slowed and his hearing sharpened as he listened. Joel held his breath hoping that Lonnie, who he'd guessed it must be, turned away. Then three taps sounded on the door.

Eventually, he would have to face Lonnie. Joel let out his breath, and inhaled again before crossing the living room to the front door. When he opened it, he caught a flash of red, fearing at first that he'd been right about Lonnie, but there was too much red, and it wasn't the right color. A half a second passed before he registered that the visitor was actually Delilah.

"Are you going to invite me in?"

His words having disappeared, Joel nodded silently and stood to the side to let her into the living room. She pushed past him, close enough for him to smell her hair. His body tightened as the scent of her filled him from the chest through his belly.

"Where have you been?" She asked the question as she took a seat on their living room couch, and he still stood, not letting the door come to a slow close. Settled in, Delilah stared at him, piercing through into his soul.

"Just went to get some breakfast."

"Not today, Joel. Bible study. You've been skipping and I haven't seen you around the church except for during the sermons doing whatever you do in that tiny alcove you sit in. You won't even make eye contact with me since... since I told you."

His eyes involuntarily scanned over her face, and the signs were impossible to miss. Delilah's eyes had sunken into their sockets, and her cheeks had thinned too. Her hair was unusually neat and had been pulled back into a bun on her head. Delilah's wrists betrayed her disease, thinner than any natural wrist should be.

"I know," she told him. "I look like a ghost. It's the treatment. The targeted one didn't work, so we have to use the — oh, never mind."

The room steeped in silence for five seconds as they kept eye contact. Joel's heart pounded in his chest as he considered what to say. He tried, and failed, to do the Lord's work, and like Job, the Lord punished him. The evidence shifted positions on the couch before him, and he felt the bile rising in the back of his throat. Raising one finger to signify that he had to go, Joel sprinted toward the bathroom, and locked the door just in time to retch into the toilet, grateful that it only held clear blue water. Joel rested his head on the cool porcelain and let the silent tears fall, uncaring whether the tears originated with the lurch in his gut or the emotional cut of having failed the Lord, and in doing so, failing Delilah.

After three minutes of vomiting, completely clearing his stomach of all of its contents and some extra, Joel wiped his mouth on the hand towel, cleaned up the best he could in the mirror, and pushed back through the doorway.

"Delilah, I'm..."

The room before him was empty. Joel glanced around quickly, looking for signs that she had been there, and had almost convinced himself that she'd been a stress-induced hallucination when he heard an unmistakable clink of the belt latch on his kit being opened. Joel pivoted toward his room and sprinted through the doorway, only to see that he was too late. Delilah stood there, holding one of his knives in her right hand and wearing a puzzled expression.

"What's all this, Joel?"

"It's..."

Joel couldn't imagine a world in which Delilah might understand that sometimes the Lord needed work done, and Joel's job was to do it. He fought the urge to tell her, knowing from the look on her face that she'd already guessed part of it, and in her mind, he turned into a monster.

Job.

"It's a project, that's all. I like knives, and I'm learning how to sharpen them. I want to start making them myself."

Delilah lifted her other hand and Joel noticed for the first time that she'd also found the injection device. He struggled to come up with an explanation as the color drained from her face.

"I always thought you were a little strange," she whispered in such a way that he couldn't tell if she was talking to him or not, even with the direct address. "But I thought you were harmless, just a little weird."

She put the knife down and pulled up the tape, examining it with now what bordered on clinical detachment. Then she asked him a question he hadn't expected.

"Why didn't you tell me?"

The question was far from the immediate rejection he'd thought he would get. Delilah should have run screaming from the room, telling everyone who she met along the way about his kit. What he should have been doing at that very moment was frantically moving from room to room, seeking a better place to hide it, so that he could lie about it when people found out.

"What?"

"Why didn't you tell me about...whatever this is? Are you going to tell me now? You have to, don't you?"

"I don't understand."

"Joel, you know I love you. You love me, even if you're weird about it. Why can't you be honest with me about what's happening in your life? Maybe I can help you deal. Why do you keep pushing me away?"

He stood motionless before her, searching for words that wouldn't sound insane. At first, she waited, patience etched into her face. As the silent seconds ticked past, the chasm between them grew, until Joel understood intuitively that it was too late. He willed his mouth to open, and words to come out, but nothing happened. Her lips changed from a patient smile to a thin line as she put the tools back into his kit.

"Fine, Joel. I know you've been spending time with Lonnie. Maybe I'll ask him instead."

Dangerous.

"No, don't do that. I'll tell you."

He spun through scenarios in his mind, trying to craft the next lie. This time she didn't wait in silence.

"Whatever. Goodbye, Joel."

He stared after her, muted by indecision, as she left his room, and he listened to the front door latch behind her.

CHAPTER 15

HE'D BEEN DISCOVERED.

The idea forced Joel awake in the early morning hours. A trickle of rain sounded in the background, accompanied only by the sounds of what few insects refused to be daunted by the weather. Delilah coursed through Joel's mind as his stomach clenched into a tight ball and he curled in on himself, closing his eyes and willing sleep to return, but it never did. He knew that the morning was still hours away since no light penetrated his window yet, and birds hadn't begun to sing. His tired eyelids squeezed together and his teeth strained against each other as he pushed at the fear, an unnamed thing that he couldn't understand.

Joel tried to convince himself that she had only seen a box with some items in it, and a handful of knives wasn't a big deal. But it wasn't just the knives that she saw. There were also the syringes, the tape, and the powders. Together these things painted an undeniable picture, and she'd hinted at the answer with her questions. Joel couldn't tell whether what scared him the most was that she might tell someone else, or that she might have already guessed herself. Her muted reaction had given him little clue.

Then there was the question of whether or not he should tell Lonnie that he'd been discovered. The man usually seemed reasonable when Joel talked with him about the Lord's work, but how far that reason went couldn't be determined in advance. Prone to fits of emotion, Lonnie's stability and patience with Joel's mistakes had limits. This misstep could be exactly the thing that broke the tie between them. Then what happened to Delilah?

These thoughts and more accosted him and tormented him for hours, until eventually the light broke through the window, and he arose from his fetal position with the weariness of a worn soldier from a trench. With groggy eyes, he took in the room in the pale glow, passing over his childhood toys and religious books on a little case that he'd had since he was eight. Most of the stuffed animals had gone away during his pre-adolescence, but a tiny orange elephant remained, perched on the shelf next to his Bible. His hands slowly went to it, and he pulled it from the shelf, knocking the Bible down as he did so. The toy offered no comfort, and he couldn't even remember the last time it had.

As he returned it to the shelf, he picked his Bible up from its side to straighten the Lord's word. It immediately fell open as he did so, split about halfway down the center. He pulled it from the shelf and examined the page where it opened, half expecting to find some guidance in this possible sign from the Lord, but as it opened to the beginning of the New Testament, something else caught his attention. A white piece of paper had been folded neatly into the book, and flattened so thin that he could have held the Bible many times, and in fact had, without ever noticing.

Joel retrieved the paper, and unfolded each thin crease carefully. He made his way to his writing desk, and placed the unfolded parchment against it, eyes misting up as he made out his father's messy scrawl. The top of the note addressed him in a way that only his father ever had, with a short abbreviation of his middle name.

——

Dear Em,

I can only imagine what my leaving must be like for you, and if I'd had more time, I would explain it all. You're so young, and when I look at you, I see me when I was your age, struggling to make sense of the world. In your eyes, I see hope and love, and at those times, I can't imagine telling you any of what I'm writing here. One day you will find this though. And when that day comes, I hope you're old enough to understand that leaving you was the most difficult decision I'd ever made in my life.

I can't tell you everything. This is for your own protection. There are things happening in the church that aren't the Lord's work. Three good friends have died in the last week, so I am a little upset as I write this. Take that into account, son, as I'm not even sure how much of what I think I know is true.

A week ago, several hundred thousand dollars disappeared from the church coffers. Vanished, gone. You may not know that the founding families of this church were us and the Reynolds. I still remember the day we found the grounds, abandoned and useless land that had once been several farms linked together. It felt like a sign from the Lord, but I'm not so sure any more.

I asked everyone in turn about it, and got only blank

*stares. You know I was pastor and that was part of my job —
keeping the church running. Nobody knew anything, but it
was only the four of us who had access to the money. We'd all
signed together for the accounts.*

*You may hear a lot of things about me when I'm gone.
Please believe that lack of faith had nothing to do with it.
What pushed me out was the look in your mother's eyes when
I asked her. She gave me that cold stare, the one that pene-
trates through to your soul. Then my friends began to get sick,
people I had confided in. Even now, as I write this, I wonder if
I may be next.*

*Probably a lot of this is in my imagination. Lord knows
that can get the best of me sometimes. But with your mother
and me, distrust has become a pastime. I don't believe at all
that your mother is involved in any of this. But what I do
know is that I don't trust her as I should, and so there's no
longer a place for me here.*

I love you, and I always will.
Dad

———

Joel kept the tears from falling down his cheeks by willpower
alone as he made out the sentences through blurry lenses. He
knew that cold stare too well, having been on the receiving
end of it so many times. He knew something that his father
didn't know though. Whether through the blindness of love
or intentional self-deception, his father's note painted a
picture of a man who stood by his wife, even in the face of
evidence. Joel knew better. He'd watched his mother steer
people out of the last of their money in the face of chronic
and fatal disease. She'd always justified every action in the

Lord's name, but he knew better. To the question of whether or not his mother could be involved in such things, his answer was undeniably yes.

And in his fury and pain, he finally felt he had the strength to confront her about it.

Joel discovered his mother in her study, flipping through documents that were either her religious notes or various highly-annotated scripture extractions. He felt the oppressiveness of the Lord's presence as he entered, surrounded as she was by His word, but he persevered, considering that if the Lord was there, whose side He was on had yet to be determined.

As he entered, her eyes flashed at him only briefly before settling back onto whatever it was that she examined. His fury grew as he recognized this for the dismissal that it was. Joel was a nobody, to her, and just an unfortunate expulsion from her loins, unworthy of her respect. He wouldn't let her ignore him this time. Joel slammed the note down before her.

"What does this mean?" Joel surprised himself with the evenness of his tone.

"Oh." She said as she grabbed the paper and tilted her head, examining his father's handwriting. "Where did you find that?"

"My Bible. I guess he meant for me to find it sooner, but you know it's been a while since I've opened a Bible."

"I know, Joel. Once you loved the Lord, and now — I don't even know if you believe anymore."

The accusation stung and he involuntarily lowered his gaze.

"I believe," he said. "I've always believed. But you? What have you been doing in the Lord's name?"

His mother sighed and pushed back from her desk, eyes

never leaving the messy script until they finally looked up and met Joel's.

"Baby boy..."

"Don't call me that."

She grimaced.

"Joel, when adults fight sometimes, they do things — mean things — to each other. If you call your father and ask him he'll tell you that note was written in anger and to ignore it."

"Funny, Mom. How should I do that? It's not like we have his number. People who *disappear* don't generally leave forwarding addresses. Come to think of it, why would he disappear? Why not just leave, like a normal, straightforward divorce?"

His mother stood slowly, staring into him the entire time. He felt apprehension or guilt tickling at his stomach, but he didn't back down.

"Your father hated me at the end," she told him. "He lost the faith, and I made him leave. I made him leave so that you could grow up in the light of the Lord."

"Or you were stealing money and hurting people."

She shook her head.

"No, Joel. I don't expect you to believe me. You've been so distant lately and you won't open up to me. I think — I think you really needed your father in your life and I took him away from you."

She tilted her head to the left and looked over his face and chest.

"You've gotten so *big*. I didn't want you to grow up without him. It's like I said, though. Adults do mean things to each other. I hated him, and when he tried to reach out to you, I blocked his number, burned the letters. I can't tell you how hard it was running a church by myself, raising a little boy and knowing nothing about what I was doing. Some day, maybe you'll see, Joel, baby boy."

He didn't correct her this time, but he didn't respond either. If he'd opened his mouth, Joel wasn't certain what might come out. He wanted to defend his father's parting accusations, and chastise her, not giving up the only advantage that he'd ever had in their relationship. But at the same time, a lump formed in his throat, and he thought he might let loose a scream on the world if his lips were to part. He sealed his mouth in a straight line, keeping his anger and fear inside. His mother took a step toward him, and Joel took a step back in response. She smiled.

"Tell me about Delilah, baby boy. Do you like her?"

"I don't want to talk about Delilah. I want to talk about Dad."

"Why should we discuss that further, Joel? You've decided I'm guilty. I just want to know if my baby boy is in love."

When she said the word love, her face slackened and softened, and her eyes went round. The smile on her face seemed suddenly genuine, as though she actually cared, and as though she hadn't tried to prevent them from being together.

"I do like her. Why don't you?"

"So many questions, Joel. I never said I don't like her. I don't like her parents. Remember how I said that adults can be cruel? When your father left, there was a hole here in this church as big as the hole in my heart. Those two, like vultures, swooped in to try to kick me out, as though they could. The church was my idea, and my tribute to the Lord.

It is my paean in celebration to the Lord and something that I created from my heart to sing His praise."

Joel's heart skipped a beat as he digested her words. Each time Lonnie did the Lord's work, he captured and sacrificed a paean in his name. And now, he heard Lonnie's words coming out of his mother's mouth. His mother must have seen his confusion all over his face.

"Joel?"

He stepped backwards and felt behind him for the door handle.

"I'm leaving."

"I don't know what else to do, baby boy. I don't want to lose you. When are you coming back? We still need to talk."

"I don't know." Joel turned and pushed his way through the door, only to realize that he'd left his father's note with the woman. Tears pushed their way from his eyes and cascaded down to his chest. He'd come for answers and left more confused than when he'd arrived. She *always* did that to him. Anyone would have known that he had less than half a chance of getting anything from her except pain.

These thoughts jumbled together with others in his mind. A certain kind of sense underpinned her words, however little he wanted to believe. In his mind, he felt the tension of the days and weeks before his father disappeared. Joel remembered the fights, and the ones that stuck with him the most were the screaming matches just before church on weekends, and how they faded into mist just before the ceremony. All smiles, all the time in front of the crowds and cameras, but the tension never left for him. For Joel, he waited in fear as the ceremony unfolded, steeped in apprehension that after it finished, the fighting would continue. Their home would once again turn into a war zone.

He stalled, standing in the hallway like a broken robot, unsure of what to do next. A moment passed and his confusion remained, then the click of the door behind him told him that his mother had come out as well. Joel turned to look at her, and he though he could make out snail-like streaks down her cheeks. How long had it been since he'd seen her cry? He couldn't remember.

"He hated me Joel. Now you know. It was the four of us once, all joy and light, and I bought this plot of land. See, it was my family who had the money, and everyone else — well, they had next to nothing, really. So I had to do it for everyone."

Joel stood in silence, checking each word for misdirection. His resolve weakened as he crossed the short distance to her, and she continued.

"I didn't put anyone else's name on the property. At first, it was because I couldn't. They'd had no credit, no connections. It would only have made it more expensive to buy. As the years passed, he hated that more and more. The wife should be submissive, he would say. 'Wives, submit to your husband as the Lord.' He grew bitter that I had control of the church and he had nothing. Then we had you."

She reached out her hand and took his, and he felt her soft fingers caress his palm.

"Then we had you — a boy who needed to become a man. You can't imagine what that did to him. Suddenly, he was an example, and a pinnacle, and yet — he wasn't the man of his own house. He began to work against me then, committed to fulfilling the vision of what the man should be. I told him, read Galatians 3:28."

Joel knew the scripture.

"There is neither Jew nor Gentile, neither slave nor free,

nor is there male and female, for you are all one in Christ Jesus."

"Exactly. We are all equal — this is the message I tried to bring to him. And I was petty. I could have added him as owner, and all of them really. I admit that was my failing. I could have done that. But he made it so *hard*."

She tugged on his hand, pulling him forward toward her, and he no longer resisted. He lost his breath for a second and then felt the lump in his throat expand, and finally work its way up into his eyes. Tears poured out as he lowered his head onto her shoulder. His mother. He felt that finally, in this one moment, she had been honest with him. She had finally told him something truthful, even if he couldn't quite understand which part of it was true, or to what degree, he could see at least that it pained her to tell him what she did, and that meant something.

"I love you, Joel," she whispered into his ear. "I'm not perfect, but I try. I really do."

"I know, Mom."

They stood in the hallway, clutching each other in the silence of their empty home. It still wasn't enough. Joel broke free from his mother's embrace and made his way out into the garden. This time, he neither sought Lonnie, who was disappointed in his inability to perform the Lord's work, or Delilah, disturbed by his desire to do so. He walked on the other side of the church, an area cluttered with yaupons with only a single trail cutting through. Gnarly pecan trees loomed over them, holding forth clusters of pecans, almost ready to fall. A few discarded green shells cluttered the sidewalk before him.

His mind turned over the events from earlier. He wondered about his father's letter, his mother's confession.

The catharsis of his mother's divulgence, and their shared tears, slowly fell from him. One thought occurred to him and wedged itself into his mind. Lonnie made people disappear, and he was really good at it. Joel couldn't remember how long Lonnie had been at the church, though he'd only been a gardener there for a couple of months. The thought turned over and over in his mind.

Had Lonnie been the reason people were disappearing? Could he have been doing that for so long?

Joel shook free of the idea, and instead focused on his immediate problem. He saw Delilah's sickly face in his mind. Somehow, he had to get the Lord's work done — it was the only way to save her. Whatever else he had learned, whatever other emotions he felt, Delilah's life hung in the balance. Maybe he wasn't Job after all, but Joshua, asking the Lord to still the sun and keep Delilah alive.

CHAPTER 16

THE DAYS WARMED as the year continued its relentless march from Spring into Summer. Evening thunderstorms decimated fields and turned the dry sand into unforgiving mud in the few areas of the churchyard where the natural terrain still claimed hold. One such area was just beyond the little gardening shed, which sat straddling the idyllic foliage on one side, kept up with excessive amounts of watering, and the dry sand on the other. Farther away stood a backdrop of marsh after a massive downward slope toward the pressing jungle beyond it. Joel took all of this in while he waited impatiently for Lonnie.

The rain stopped and the sun now clung to the sky and re-heated the lukewarm air back to stifling. Joel's t-shirt, soaked first with rain, now ran with sweat. The gardening shed that claimed Joel's attention was locked tight.

"Mr. Joel?" He heard Lonnie's voice come from behind him near the left side of the shed from where he stood. Turning slowly, he saw Lonnie, looking as drenched as he was.

"Lonnie, we need to talk."

"Sure, Mr. Joel. That's fine. Come in?"

Joel cleared the mud and followed Lonnie around the building to its front, where he retrieved his key from his pocket and unlocked the door to swing it inward. Joel entered after the red-haired man.

"What can I do for you, sir?"

"I've been training all this time to do the Lord's work. But so far, all I've done since I got here was listen to you talk and follow people around. I *know* that the Lord's work still needs to be done. When am I going to do it?"

The words came out quickly, in rapid fire succession, and he closed his mouth afterwards, taking the time to reload his mind.

"And you believe you're ready, Mr. Joel?"

"Stop calling me that. You said I was. You said we were going to change our approach. Then it was only more of the same — waiting and watching. I'm ready, Lonnie."

"Every time you go out, something goes wrong."

At least Lonnie didn't work around the edges. He got to exactly what Joel thought — no confidence.

"This isn't the real thing, Lonnie. Following people through the city? All that does is put me at risk the longer we do it. We just need to get out there get it done. In and out, there won't be a problem. I can handle it."

"You didn't last time."

"I didn't get the chance. With you following me around, and stepping in, I never will. I've got to do it on my own."

As the words came out, Joel's breath sucked away and he seized up as his jaw clamped shut. He felt his eyes go wider, and hoped that Lonnie couldn't see the fear that now clouded them. Joel didn't want to kill anyone. Delilah *needed* him to. She was wasting away, and following people around wasn't making her better. Lonnie stared at him but didn't seem to notice — or if he did he didn't react.

"Fair point, Mr. Joel. Fair point. Okay."

"Okay?"

"Yep. Remember that man that you tracked before? It's time to bring him in. I was out checking to see if anything's changed with him just now and it doesn't seem so. Same routine as always. If you want to do something on your own, why don't you take your kit and go see if you can get him back here?"

After his outburst, Joel could only agree despite the anxiety pressing at his mind. He nodded his head slowly up and down. His heart raced as he realized the repercussions of all that he'd just agreed to. But, he had to remember, it was for Delilah.

"I will. And he will be my paean, *my* offering to the Lord."

"We'll see. First you got to get him here don't you?"

That part at least was true.

Half an hour later, Joel arrived at the man's house to find it just as he remembered. The sun now dropped nearly to the horizon and cast a shadow from the skinny modern home across the yard, falling just short of where Joel had parked the volantrae on the shoulder. He thought through his process from training in his head. Quick, innocent conversation — perhaps asking for directions. Then...

Then what? He realized that he hadn't actually been on a kidnapping yet, and all he had done was follow. The idea occurred to him that Lonnie had told him to go so that he realized how little he actually knew about the process. It was possible that Lonnie expected him to return empty-handed.

Joel wouldn't do that. He would have a quick, innocent conversation, and then... hit the man with a hammer. He had one of those in his kit, but he hadn't known what it was for. This must be its purpose. A quick hit with the hammer would send the man down, and hopefully would render him unconscious. Yet exactly how hard to hit someone with a hammer and not kill them Joel didn't know. He sucked in his breath and consoled himself that the man was slated to die anyway, so it wouldn't be too much of a problem if the hammer swung a little harder than it should. What he didn't know was whether the Lord would still count the man without all of the ritual.

The hammer would have to do. His only other choice from the kit were his knives, and he didn't yet know how to do more than flip them around. Joel guessed that it would be much more difficult to render someone unconscious with them. His eyes slid over the syringe. He knew what that was for.

He steeled himself with a single thought: for Delilah.

Joel stepped from the volantrae and out into the humidity. Sweat immediately filled his eyes and soaked his clothes for a third time. He blinked to clear them as he crossed the street with his hammer clutched between shaking fingers. An approaching car made him transfer the hammer to his left hand, to use his body for concealment. He swung open the iron gate, listening to its creaking sound announce his presence to anyone who could hear. But he wouldn't fail. Joel walked up past the dandelion-filled grass, and to the front door. The bottom hinge hung on for dear life as the door rested canted in its frame. He hadn't noticed that before. The car, the dilapidated house, the unkept yard — all of it indicated that the man was poor and a nobody. He wondered briefly how this man could have offended the Lord, but shook the thought from his mind.

And suddenly Joel found himself on the doorstep. With a trembling hand, he waved at the sensor to announce his presence. Listening intently, Joel heard no sounds coming from within. The silence dripped by and his face felt hot with the awareness that around him, the neighborhood continued by, with casual glances through windows and passers by capturing his image. His heart beat quickened and more perspiration gathered on his forehead as he heard the door finally click open. The man's face appeared in the narrow gap.

"Can I help you?"

By this point, the nervous energy had stolen Joel's reserve, and he stood there, looking foolish and stared at his paean. He realized that in his heightened agitation, the man's name escaped him, so he couldn't even fake the introduction he had planned. His body reacted more quickly than his mind and the hammer swung up of its own accord and connected with the man's face, indenting it right between the man's eyes, and the man fell so quickly that Joel was certain he'd killed him. Joel pushed on the door, only to discover that the body now blocked it. He shoved with all his might, and felt the man's body slide inward as the gap opened. Then, once inside, Joel let out a sigh and closed the door behind him.

No other sounds in the house. That was good.

He peaked out through the window beside the front door shoving the curtains aside, and gasped at the distance from where he now stood to where the volantrae was located across the street. Somehow, he had to get the man there without anyone noticing. Joel glanced at the other homes, and saw no movement. He could make it if he could get there quickly enough *right that second*. But then, a kid on a scooter rode by — a child young enough that Joel sought for a parent chasing him until the boy pulled into a yard across the street and let himself into a home there. He must have been older than he looked.

Joel would never make it unnoticed while pulling the full-grown man he could barely shove across the floor. He needed another plan. But first, he checked the man's breathing, and felt a faint rasp in and out on the back of his hand. Good because the man needed to be alive for the ceremony. Bad because he now had to worry if the man would awaken at some point. Leaving the door ajar a few inches, Joel made his way back to his volantrae alone to retrieve his kit. The ventilation tape would do the job of keeping the man restrained, awake or not. The first thing he taped was the man's mouth, stuck in a drooling grin soon hidden behind a thick layer of gray. He then pulled the man's hands together and taped them, followed by the legs. Only after that did his anxiety start to wane. He was in control of the situation.

Joel turned his attention to getting the man out of the house. Though he couldn't make it to his volantrae across the street, he could, he thought, make it down the sidewalk as far as the man's car on the near side. Searching through the man's pockets — difficult as the man's clothes were too small and the pockets had flattened against his skin — Joel eventually located keys that he thought had to be to the vehicle. These he placed in his own pockets, hoping the keys would be detected in the proximity of the vehicle in the same way that newer cars and volantrae detected biometrics. Then, taking a deep breath, he grabbed the man's arms, and pulled as hard as he could away from the door.

The man didn't budge.

Joel's stomach dropped.

His eyes scanned the foyer but found nothing to assist him. Then he ran toward the back of the house on the same level, but all he found was broad wooden flooring. Downstairs, he saw what looked like an office. But when he went to the back porch, he saw something that stopped him in his tracks.

A toy wagon. It wasn't a levitating one that relied on magnetic propulsion to stay afloat, but a classic wagon with wheels and everything. At the moment it was cluttered with toys. Joel gulped hard and his breath stopped before he clenched his teeth, pushed through the doorway, and dumped the toys over the back porch. After carrying the wagon back to the foyer, he shoved the man hard out of the way, and swung the door open. Then he poked his head through and surveyed the surroundings, seeing nobody around, even in the many facing windows. He lined the wagon up with the walkway, and worked to get the man onto it. Even when the man's mass finally centered over the rickety child's toy, the man's leggs dragged on the ground, but it was the best Joel could do.

Joel then circled behind the wagon, knelt into a runner's starting position and placed his hands on the toy. He checked his alignment one more time, took a deep breath, and shoved the wagon over the barricade, only to have it tumble down the steps and deposit the large man in the yard. Joel sprinted after him, making enough noise that Joel felt it might awaken the entire neighborhood. He struggled to his feet and righted the wagon, then spent another five minutes leveraging the man's portions over the wheels again. Looking up, the streets were still empty, though the parallel skyway had begun to take traffic.

Joel shoved the wagon again, and this time it sailed true, right through the gate and slammed into the side of the man's car, before bouncing back and in the process somehow shifting sideways, lining the wheels up with the gradient of the hill. As the wheels slowly began to turn, Joel caught up to the wagon and placed himself against it, taking a deep breath as it stopped. Then he popped open the back door to the man's car, and shoved him inside. As soon as the man lay in the seat, Joel heard the sound of wheels accelerating, and turned in time to see the wagon disappearing down the hill. He slammed the door shut and skirted around to the driver's side door, which he yanked open, and deposited himself in the front seat.

"Start."

Nothing happened. He examined the dashboard and discovered a button labeled start then pushed it. With a little trial and error, Joel managed to free himself from the parking spot and onto the empty street. It wasn't until he reached the first stoplight that he let out his breath and felt a sense of relief settle over him.

He'd done it. And when he made it back to the church, Lonnie would have to admit that he'd succeeded. More importantly, even the Lord couldn't deny him this paean.

An hour later, because roads were just so much slower than the skyways, Joel arrived back at the church campus. He circled the complex, driving around its perimeter on the side streets, until he found the little delivery road used to bring in supplies. This he followed up until the branch that led to the back of the little shed. He hopped out and made his way around to the front, just in time to see Lonnie stepping out through the door.

"Mr. Joel?"

The man's features carried a surprise in his arched eyebrows and open-mouthed stare.

"Come help me," Joel told him, nodding with his head toward where he'd left the car.

When he met Lonnie's eyes again, he saw that Lonnie understood and kicked open the front door to as wide as it could get. The two of them managed to get the man inside without further incident, and a few minutes later, the man lay strapped to the table. Joel retrieved his tools from the car and set them next to the man on the stretcher as Lonnie brought the man to wakefulness by waving something under his nose. Joel closed and latched the door.

"It's time for you to repent," Lonnie said, as the man's eyes darted back and forth between Joel and Lonnie. "The Lord has found you wanting. You speak out against His good name and tarnish and stain the reputation of His loyal followers."

Lonnie began to walk to the man's side, as he examined the man's neck. Then, slowly, Lonnie walked to his kit and retrieved the syringe. This he loaded from one of the bottles of fluid, and he walked toward the man.

"Lord, accept this paean to Your majesty. He has spoken against You and so here, we delivery him back to Your Grace. Amen."

"Let me," Joel told Lonnie, as he stepped between Lonnie and the man. Lonnie pushed him aside and ignored him.

"Lonnie, I *have* to do it."

Lonnie, now a man possessed, brandished his syringe

before the man, staring with unseeing eyes.

Delilah.

Joel reached back into his kit, and pulled out a knife before he knew what he was doing. He sprinted before Lonnie, and in one quick motion, drew the blade across the man's neck. Barely had he finished when he felt Lonnie's body collide with his, sending him reeling into the floor of the shed. The paean's blood spilled down on top of them, and Joel felt warm fluid spread in short bursts across his chest. With a quick roll, both of them were clear of the blood but collided with a far counter, sending Lonnie's tools down atop them. As quickly as the struggle had begun, it stopped, with Lonnie standing up beside him, and dusting his clothes off with his hands while spreading the no-longer life-sustaining fluid over his jeans.

"The Lord..." Lonnie began, but then stopped as his eyes went wide at the site of the mess they had caused.

"The Lord got his offering," Joel said, filling the silence with his own ambitions. "And He got it from me."

Lonnie looked at Joel with those same wide eyes, as if he barely recognized him. Then his eyes narrowed, and he stepped backwards along the counter's length.

"I suppose, Mr. Joel. But now, look at that."

Joel turned from his position on the floor, still not fully recovered from the short fall. Blood was everywhere, falling in thick streams from the counter.

"Someone will have to clean this," Lonnie said, in a way that let Joel know exactly who that somebody was. Joel's only response was to nod as Lonnie turned from him, and made his exit.

There, alone with a corpse slowly emptying itself of fluid, Joel felt the impact of what he had done.

The words *thou shalt not kill* now furrowed into his brain.

His stomach churned and he bowled over to wretch, but nothing came out. His body heaved in the dim lighting over and over, and he struggled to right himself. It had been necessary. This he told himself repeatedly, but his body didn't believe him. His urge to vomit only grew until finally he forced out a thin stream of bile, and lay defeated on the floor covered in filth.

The Lord works in mysterious ways. Joel knew this was true, and all he had to do was believe and have faith. He reached for redemption from his crumpled mass on the floor, grasping with his emotions for anything he could find. As usual, he felt nothing but the encroaching silence broken by the distant sound of the stolen car pulling away. Gasping for breath, he realized that he'd forgotten about that part of the clean-up. Lonnie, as insane as he seemed, always remembered. He doubted anyone would ever find that vehicle again once Lonnie was done. And somehow, he had to do the same with a body.

Hours later, Joel had discovered that bandaging the wound stopped the bleeding and a bleach scrub could handle most of the blood. There were still specks here and there, but he would get those later. His stomach still threatened to spill its contents, but he pushed through. When Lonnie returned to help cut up the body, Joel couldn't stay in the same room.

"You'll get there, Mr. Joel. Go home. I'll handle the rest."

Joel grimaced as he made his way to the door and wondered if the offering had been enough. Catching sight of the man's partially-dismembered body, Joel felt the color drain from his face. If this wasn't enough, Joel didn't know how he would be able to help Delilah now.

CHAPTER 17

JOEL HAD SLEPT LESS than fifteen hours over the next three days. Images of the dying man's face ravaged his dreams and seeped into his waking hours. The sordid act of the little he'd seen of dismembering the body left the rest to his overactive imagination. He caught flashes of Lonnie burying the pieces in various parts of the church garden in the dark of night. He hadn't seen Lonnie since that night and he wasn't sure how Lonnie felt about him after their fight. At the morning's sermon, there was a noticeable gap in the front where the man had previously gyrated to each hymn.

Joel examined Delilah, watching her from his tech support booth, analyzing each movement for improvement. She'd lost the ability to dance, nor did she sing with the rest of the worshipers. Her normal demeanor had been replaced by a vacant stare, and a thick wool cap that seemed out of place in the heat. He only realized how fervently he fixated on her when she returned his gaze along with a thin, weak smile. In that, he saw no strength, but he reminded himself that the Lord worked in mysterious ways. From where he stood, Joel couldn't tell much more than that Delilah was on her own two feet. He decided he needed a closer look and motioned toward the back with his eyes. Her subtle nod told him that she would meet him, and again skip Bible study, regardless of the risk.

Alone, in the garden, by their usual bench, they sat in silence. The heat dripped off of them, but he alone seemed to feel it. Even beneath the wool cap, Delilah's forehead displayed none of the thick beads of sweat that dripped down the sides of his face. She said nothing, and Joel — not the one for starting conversation — also said nothing. Instead he watched her face.

Her pale cheeks had hollowed out and her fingers seemed more waifish than ever as they intermingled with his knuckles. The time seemed to pass slowly as they sat there unperturbed. Once, Joel's mother approached nearby, but even she kept her reproachful nature contained, and only watched them quietly as she passed. Delilah's pale, freckled cheeks had hollowed more, and her buoyant grin had disappeared. She finally spoke with an annoyed twang to her voice.

"Why are you staring at me like that?"

"Like what?"

"Like I might fade away, or disappear. I'm not going anywhere. This is just the treatment, Joel. This is what it does. It redirects your energy to focus on fighting the disease."

"How do you feel?"

It was perhaps the stupidest question he'd ever asked, but staring at her was getting him nowhere. She pulled her fingers back from his and snapped at him.

"How do you *think* I feel, Joel? I'm dying, and the thing

that's supposed to save me is destroying my body. How do you think that makes me feel?"

"I only meant... do you feel any better today than yesterday?"

She turned her gaze from the empty garden before them to his own face.

"I see," she said, her eyes dropped. "You're holding out on some hope that I might get better. What, you don't think *prayer* is enough?"

He didn't respond to her sarcasm, but if he had responded, he'd have told her that if he thought prayer was anywhere near enough, he wouldn't have just killed a person in the garden shed.

"I don't want you to die."

She put her fingers back through his again, and clutched tightly.

"Me neither."

For the next half an hour, they sat like that, staring empty stares into the garden with him hoping desperately that his actions were enough. The Lord worked in mysterious ways.

A cool breeze drifted across and when it departed, took with it the anxiety and nervous energy that had saturated the air around them. Joel could breath again, and he sucked in a deep lungful of oxygen, letting it out slowly over several seconds. Then he turned his head toward Delilah and saw that she now watched him the way that he had been watching her. His pulse ratcheted up again as he met her green eyes.

"Joel, what was in that box?"

His efforts to control his body fell short as he lurched and felt his hand disconnect from hers. Joel turned his head away to focus instead on the paved path they'd taken to arrive at the bench, imagining running away down it, escaping her scrutiny. Instead, he decided to play dumb.

"What box?"

"The toolbox in your room. What was the syringe for?"

The air had stilled. In place of the welcoming breeze, Joel felt only the admonishing rays of the sun beating against his face, his shoulders, and his back. Even the reflected rays from the pavement were like a thousand tiny punches against his skin. He sucked in his breath.

"That shouldn't have been in there," he lied, something that he was getting better at now that he'd had the practice.

"What about the knives? You know what it looked like to me, Joel?"

He shook his head, teeth clenched and muscles drawn tight in his face, as he awaited her judgment.

"When I was little," she began, "my dad thought that I would like hunting. He has a box like that, with knives and laser cartridges and deer bait. It's gross."

Joel shuddered at that, feeling her condemnation flow past her reminiscences and into the present. He said nothing in response, and after a second's pause, Delilah continued after sucking in a breath.

"I didn't like it at all," she said. "What did deer do to us that we would want to kill them? And there are so few left since climate change anyway — do we really need to make the rest die off? But that didn't look like a deer kit that you had. You can't get close enough to a deer to use a syringe."

She paused again, this time looking at him so hard that he could feel her eyes drilling into the side of his cheek.

"I was just thinking," she continued. "They found Franklin Thomas' body the other day. Looks like he was given something — something through a syringe. Parishioners from his congregation are coming out about his pedophilia predilections. Did you know that he's abused over fifty children in that congregation? Nobody knew about it because only the one person talked about it — until he died."

Joel still said nothing, because there was nothing to say. He still had nightmares about Franklin Thomas's darting eyes coming to a slow stop, washing over him with that silent plea for help.

"If someone had done that, they'd need a syringe. And they'd need knives. That got me thinking that maybe..."

She didn't continue, but broke off her words and looked on him in silence. Then she forced her fingers back between his. A strange kind of light shimmered behind her gaze, the only part of her that had any fire left. With his free hand, Joel wiped sweat from the back of his neck.

"It's just a toolbox. Mom gave me those knives a long time ago — seemed like as good a place to keep them as any."

Pain rose in him with the same intensity that the fire left.

"Yeah, I guess so," she said. "Joel, there's something else I have to tell you."

So far, their entire conversation had been her telling him things. Normally, he loved to hear her go on and on about her experiences, often imagining what it would be like living a life like hers instead of one which tethered him to the church grounds and his mother. But today, her questions had shaken him, and he didn't know if he could take more questioning. Still, he had no good way to stop her, and if she had the energy to speak, he committed himself to letting her while also not giving anything away.

"Tomorrow I have an operation," she said. "This one is a big one. The treatment has killed most of the stray cancer cells in my blood, they think. But the mass in my brain —

that's not shrinking. They have to operate to get it out before it does more damage."

Joel bit his lip.

"There's only a sixty-percent survival rate for the new treatment. Mom says if it doesn't work, well, then I'm scared, Joel."

His arm began to shake and he forced it to still. Then he pulled his fingers from Delilah's thin hand and lay his arm over her shoulders, squeezing her close to him as she lay her head against him.

"Don't worry, Delilah," he told her in as confident a voice as he could muster. "I'm sure it will go well."

"I might die, Joel," she repeated the thought in a voice that wavered and trembled before falling off.

"And you might not. The Lord will provide."

Joel had done his part yet he felt no more confident now than he had before he'd done the Lord's work. A tiny voice inside of him questioned whether the work that he had done, or that Lonnie had done, originated from the Lord or from some other source. He forced the voice to silence, as the deed had been completed, and the moment of trial was before them. Delilah's operation would be the test, and if she didn't make it, then he would know that his relationship with the Lord had not only not improved, but had deteriorated so much that he could no longer be sure he even had a place in the church at all.

But that was his problem, and the operation, as much as he wanted control over it, wasn't about him. It was about Delilah.

"Do you have an animus module?"

Joel asked the question as though he were an expert, but he'd only heard about them. She shook her head against his neck, as he had suspected. The device could help keep her consciousness safe so if her body died, she might be able to someday have another. She didn't have one. His own mother had raged every other sermon about their unnaturalness, and that no god-fearing person would have one put in their body. The soul was part of the body, and that couldn't go hopping around on a technical implant that could be backed up and restored somewhere else. Humans shouldn't play god. For most of his life, he'd believed her, but today he wished with all of his heart that Delilah had one, and if he had to guess, her parents probably wished the same. He began to suspect that his mother had been wrong about a lot of things she'd told him.

He lay his head over the top of Delilah's, taking in her smell, now perfume-less. She didn't smell like flowers at all now, but some combination of salt and musk with a tinge of chemicals. The fragrance of her was at the same time familiar and distant, like he'd known her his entire life, and yet had only just now discovered her.

CHAPTER 18

JOEL DIDN'T SLEEP that evening, for a multitude of reasons, the most prominent being that Delilah's operation loomed large in his imagination. Every fifteen minutes it seemed that his mind took the journey to a medical room with her laying unconscious on a table. In some imaginings, he had been convinced that the body he'd seen was her corpse, as it lay immobile with arms hanging uselessly down from the table. Each such experience brought his fetal position in tighter, but none made his gut wrench more than when his concern over her safety merged with his fear of his own emerging darkness.

By the time the morning came, he'd soaked through his sheets and the little sleep that he'd gotten had been in short spurts between nightmares and dark visions of the future. Against this backdrop, he welcomed the sunlight that brought him safety from his dreams even if it meant his attempts at rest had come to an end.

Sunday service was an empty ritual without Lonnie

gyrating or Delilah's slow swaying to take his attention away from the sermon and the crowds that worshiped him and his mother almost as much as they did the Lord they served. Or, who both of them claimed to serve, she in her infantile devotional way, committed regardless of consequence and past all point of reason. He, in his own lost-son sort of way, struggling to find his way back. Both seeking the Lord's light, a light that he now suspected would never be found in the masses of hysterical, screaming church-fans. Joel shut his eyes against them, all of them, but he couldn't close off his ears, and his mother's sermon pounded them for a solid hour, covering the same themes as always.

"What do you suggest to someone who comes to you to tell them that something is lacking from their life? Someone whose life is incomplete?"

The question hung out in the crowd for only a second before screams began in their canned response. There was only one right answer — seek the Lord. Every question had the same answer, in fact.

"We all know this. So what do we tell someone who is happy in their life, and who the Lord has blessed? Do we tear them down or do we strive to emulate their example?"

Joel translated the question in his mind: *when you see us, in this house larger than any that you will ever own, with more and better volantrae, clean and pressed clothing, all of those benefits at the expense of your tithes, it is only because we are blessed that we have so much. Don't judge us the same way as others, don't be jealous of our success. This can be you, too, if only you have a little more faith. The Lord provides.*

He stopped listening. The words still cut through into his head, but he turned them around and sent them on their way without processing. Joel could give all of his mother's sermons by heart anyway.

Toward the end of the sermon, the door in the back of the room cracked, letting in light and capturing Joel's attention as well as that of half of the audience. Through the opening stumbled a tall figure, who Joel couldn't make out at first, until the door swung to a close behind him. Then he saw the face, the wide grin beneath curly red hair. It was Lonnie Lloyd Simpson, and he was working his way toward the front of the room, toward his usual spot. The crowd parted as though they all recognized him and the danger he posed, but when he arrived, the path closed up behind him, and the crowd began to sway again as though nothing happened.

But his mother stuttered.

She only did it once, and Joel was probably the only one who heard, but she clearly stuttered, something that his refined mother never did. She practiced her sermons so relentlessly that they all had been broken down and were hobbled into being her willing servants, yet in this one case, Lonnie's entrance had shaken her. Then Joel remembered seeing her the day before hurrying past him and Delilah in the direction of the gardener's shed. And the day before that, moving quickly in the same direction.

Something clicked in his mind at that point, but it was something he couldn't believe so he tried to dismiss the thought as readily as it arrived. *She and Lonnie worked together doing the Lord's work.* No, that could never be true. But then, where did he get his instructions from. Was it a coincidence that Franklin Thomas had died after that dinner with his mother? But that would mean that his mother, lacking in all self-awareness but not in empathy, had to be working with Lonnie. Joel tried to envision his mother passing a list of transgressors to Lonnie. He suspected it wouldn't happen that way though. With Lonnie's ambition, his mother would only have to complain in his presence.

"Those who claim they do the Lord's work, do they really? If their lives don't reflect his bounty, you can be sure they do not."

The lecture broke through for a moment, and what she said chilled him. Her own success justified any actions she might perform, *they* might perform. He was complicit as well so he couldn't judge her too harshly. If Delilah survived the operation, he would still carry the guilt of the killings he'd witnessed and in which he'd participated. Whatever the Lord did to Lonnie to purify his soul seemed not to work for Joel. The guilt clung to his shoulders like a lead-lined shroud.

The sermon ended, and people began to exit. With a few keystrokes, Joel closed down the virtual conference, careful to mentally record the numbers. Over a million logins, most of which stayed for the entire sermon, had occurred that morning. A good number of those were former Dallas parishioners who, upon learning the truth about Franklin, sought out a new home for their religious needs. His mother would love to hear about that.

After the sermon, he recused himself into his room, turned out the lights, and lay prone in bed, counting the minutes until Delilah's operation. He didn't know exactly when it would be, but he knew it would be some time in the afternoon, so he'd picked 2:00 PM. The sermon let out at 11:00 AM, and he intended to lay there immobile for the entire three hours or until he heard the news about her outcome. Then three rapid knocks tapped at the door, hard enough to be heard, but light enough to be ignored if he tried. Then they came again. With slow deliberation he rose from his bed and made his way to the door. There he saw his mother, face beaming, leaning forward as though she might come in, even though he hadn't asked her to. Sure enough, she pressed past him and into his room, prompting him to slide his eyes over to the edge of his bed, where his toolbox sat beneath the frame.

"A million, Joel. And most of them stayed and most of them gave. We made over two million dollars today alone!"

"You mean the Lord made?"

His mother, who had raced past him, now turned to face him.

"Yes, of course. Is that what I said?"

"You said *we*."

"I meant us and the Lord, Joel. Are you okay? No, of course you're not. I'm sorry. Delilah?"

He sighed and sidestepped her, making his way back to his empty bed, then sitting on the edge of it.

"Nothing's wrong. Just you said *we*. We are doing the Lord's work, right?"

"She'll be okay, Joel. Her parents are regular donors to the church, and the Lord sees that. He'll take care of her."

"I told you I'm fine," he said, cringing at the edge to his voice and aware that protesting in the way he was didn't convey the message of his words. But it was enough to make her back down.

"Okay, you're fine." She said it in a monotone that told him she didn't really believe it, but wouldn't ask again. Then, as quickly as she'd asked, she moved back to the subject of her crowd size.

"Over a million, Joel. That's got to be a record! And I couldn't have done it without you. Thank you, Joel, for all of your help."

More than you know, he thought, and he nodded, acknowledging her compliment in a sullen way that he'd hoped clued her to leave. Sure enough, she turned, leaving the room and him in silence to be tormented by his thoughts alone.

CHAPTER 19

DESPITE HIS SHOWING ON SUNDAY, Monday morning arrived without Joel ever having an opportunity to talk to the man. Lonnie was the only person with whom he could talk about the feelings that plagued him from their combined work. Surely Lonnie had felt the way Joel did at some point in his life. Joel wanted to know how Lonnie got past the guilt. But Lonnie never came. Worse than that, he heard no news of Delilah's operation at all that day. He didn't even know if she'd had the operation. As short a walk as it was over to Delilah's house, Joel couldn't make himself take the trip because *what if she had died?*

Exhausted from two sleepless nights, Joel wandered the grounds on auto-pilot, allowing his feet to carry him wherever they wanted, which may have been a mistake. It seemed that they wanted to go to the gardener's shed, where he was sure he would find Lonnie sharpening his tools or transplanting some exotic plant that really shouldn't be grown in Texas, but that his mother couldn't live without.

The shack looked less menacing during the daylight than

it had in his mind since the incident. The nondescript building looked exactly like a gardener's shed should, with thick green walls and a single white door that beckoned entry. With a shrug, he took two steps toward the door and gave a quick twist to the handle. As it opened before him, he took a step backward, but then swallowed and willed himself through.

"Mr. Joel!"

The greeting contained so much excitement that Joel's lips curled into a smile without his thinking about it. He forced the corners of his lips back down into a thin line and nodded to Lonnie.

"Mr. Joel, I've been traveling. Went up to Dallas. It turns out, there were a few others involved in the pedophile thing. I've been cleaning it up a bit, if you can understand. Paeans a-plenty."

The thought made Joel's stomach start to reject the contents of his morning snack, and he forced it back down.

"How many?" Joel asked the question without wanting to know the answer. He didn't want to know, but he *needed* to know. The scales in his head were balancing the lives taken, the lives destroyed, and the net good to the world, which he quantified by the children who had lived under the shadow of abuse.

"Only five," Lonnie said, with something that Joel perceived of as an air of disappointment.

"How many were you expecting?"

"Twenty or so, but five is good. They won't be bothering anyone anymore. Oh, I heard the good news about your little girlfriend."

Joel's face grew hot, and he clenched his teeth behind his non-smile.

"She's not my girlfriend."

"Mr. Joel, if you say so. Delilah, right? Reynolds? Anyway, she's made it through the operation and she's doing well now. Seems like she'll make a full recovery."

"How did you find out?"

Lonnie smiled and his eyes twinkled.

"I have my ways," he said. "Are you here for the next job? Don't know it yet. Won't until this afternoon, most likely."

Joel barely heard his words over the beating of his own heart at Delilah's recovery. Lonnie was a lot of things, but Joel hadn't found him to be a liar. If he said Delilah was in recovery, then she was in recovery and things were looking good. And the subtext of all of *that* was that the Lord had come through for him. The mental image of the man's dismembered body began to fade in Joel's mind as he turned that thought over. The Lord listened, and the Lord gave, yet inside, within his heart, Joel didn't find the Lord. He found a longing for Delilah, and the same self-revulsion that he'd felt before. At least this killing had been justified, and Delilah's life had been spared. If self-loathing was his sacrifice for that gift, then he would gladly pay it time and again.

The door sprang open and his mother walked through the opening. Her eyes went first to Lonnie, and then to Joel, and then back again. Joel could tell from her furrowed eyebrows of concentration that she tried to make sense of the two of them in this gardener's shed together. She shook her head, then her eyes went wide. Joel followed her eyes and saw Lonnie's toolbox, opened on the counter, tools strewn everywhere. The man had been in the process of cleaning them, Joel realized, and it was impossible to hide the rust-colored blood coating the blades of two of the knives.

"Mom, I..."

She ignored him.

"Lonnie, what's going on here?"

"Mr. Joel came in while I was cleaning up. We're just chatting."

"Lonnie, what are you chatting *about*?"

It was Joel's turn to be shocked as he turned to where his mother stood, expecting to see her reaction change from shock to disgust, but her eyes settled and her jaw muscles unclenched beneath the surface of her skin. Then Joel's attention turned to Lonnie, who smiled and winked.

"Nothing," Lonnie said, and Joel's mother exhaled and her eyes turned downward. "The weather."

She turned to Joel, seeming to suspect that Lonnie wasn't being entirely truthful — which Joel gathered was likely due to the blood-covered knives still on the table.

"What were you talking about?"

"N-nothing," Joel said, echoing Lonnie. He couldn't stop his voice from wavering.

"Lying is a sin before the Lord," she told him, her voice taking on a familiar hostile edge. "Tell me the truth."

At that point, Joel looked from Lonnie, to the tools, to his mother, and back again to the tools. He hadn't even pretended to be shocked at them, and it was too late now. The "game" was up. He grit his teeth and didn't respond.

"How long?"

"About—," began Lonnie, only to be interrupted by a rising hand.

"I asked Joel."

Joel gulped.

"A while. Since Franklin."

"You were part of that?" She turned her attention to

Lonnie. "I thought I told you not to include my son in what you were doing."

"I may do the Lord's work when you ask for it, Evie. I *don't* control the boy. He wanted to for some reason, so I let him. It's as simple as that. The Lord works in mysterious ways."

"No he doesn't," Joel's mother replied. "He tells *me* what he wants, and we make it happen. The Lord didn't want Joel wrapped up in this."

"Of course he did, or he wouldn't have brought Joel to me. He brought Joel to me the same way he brought me to you."

"The Lord had nothing to do with that. I needed work done, and I found you. Need I remind you that I also *saved* you from your addiction and from the police. You're only free because of me."

That seemed to shake Lonnie's confidence, as his smile disappeared and his eyebrows came down.

"The Lord saved me, not you. And I'm here because *He* wills it."

"Joel's not."

"I'm here because *I* will it, Mom," Joel said. "How long have you been killing people, anyway?"

"Hush, keep your voice down. It carries now that it's gotten so deep. Do you want people passing by to hear?"

"That you've been assassinating people? I don't care. My reason for being here has nothing to do with either of you. The Lord has work to do, so I do it."

He spit out the words with contempt and confidence, only one of which correctly represented the rise in his heartbeat and the tension building behind his eyes.

"*You* do it?"

His mother's face scrunched into an angry scowl and she directed the hostility toward Lonnie.

"You've made my son into a *murderer?*"

"A soldier for the Lord, Evie. Just like me, remember?"

The twinkle in Lonnie's eye and the way he cut the last syllable off made the words seem like a challenge thrown out, one which Joel's mother, in all of her fury, seemed unwilling to meet as she changed the subject.

"Joel," she started, then looked at him and closed her lips while her eyes misted over.

Joel stared at her, watching from afar as though he were watching a holovision show. Lonnie looked like a villain, with his smirks and subtle amusement for no particular reason that Joel could find. His mother, the wronged maiden. But these roles were too obvious, and his mother overplayed hers. A dispassionate observer, he watched as they both went through the motions and vied for his affections. In disgust, he turned and made his way back out through the doorway, hearing their shouts escalate toward one another, and soaking in the blood of the murders that he'd witnessed, and the one he'd committed.

Nothing about this seemed like the Lord's work anymore, but he clung to Delilah's recovery as evidence that some amount of righteousness remained in him despite his mistakes.

CHAPTER 20

AS HE CROSSED the length of the church campus, weaving along cement paths in the morning sun, the magnitude of what he'd just discovered simmered in his chest. His mother, the matron of the church, sanctioned hits against others. This idea painted Franklin Thomas under a different light. A million more members. In only a few weeks. Then his mind latched onto the ex-church member who had maligned the church on the national news, his botched job. Suddenly what they'd been doing seemed less like the Lord's work, and more like eliminating the competition and preserving the church's image. These thoughts followed him like a boulder tied to his shoulder blades as he approached the edge of the campus, tears pulling forward in his eyes. His purpose, gone in just so many seconds. The only good thing, and he wasn't certain that this was even because of anything he'd done anymore, was Delilah's recovery.

Joel realized as he emerged from the church garden's out into the neighborhood that Delilah was the force that drove his feet, and his heart pulled him along the rest of the way toward her door as he saw her home emerge before him. He bit his lip as he reached his hand up to touch the doorbell. Anxiety slowed his hand and willpower alone depressed the button all the way in. The chime echoed through the house. For a few seconds after, he listened for the rustling that would tell him that someone had actually heard, but that was silly. Delilah wouldn't be there the day after having her head cut open, and the family would be with her at the hospital. Just as he was about to turn away, the door crept open silently to reveal Delilah's mother, frazzled hair and eyes reddened for lack of sleep.

"Joel?"

He said nothing. Joel wanted to ask for Delilah, but the words wouldn't come. He struggled to convince himself that Delilah would want to see him, too. The only thing that came to his mind, in spite of all of the moments they'd shared in the garden, was the exchange the last time he'd seen her. His toolbox, now pushed so far under his bed that it couldn't be seen without crawling along the ground in his room, still existed. Her prying questions and his responses had been dry and clinical, outweighed by the pressing attestation of her impending surgery. Now, perhaps, he would hear what she really thought, and how much she believed her own musings. Now he had to decide how much lying he would do. But lying to her wasn't something he wanted, and it only made him think of his mother's collusion with Lonnie and the lies and half-truths he'd gotten from both of them.

"I'm glad your here. Delilah will want to see you."

"She's here?"

Mrs. Reynolds nodded.

"You remember where her room is?"

Joel nodded and stepped past her, taking the stairs just

behind and to her left one slow step at a time, each one tempting him to turn and descend again. But, he mused, eventually they would have to talk. And he wanted, or needed, proof that her recovery was going well.

He paused outside of her door. For a second again he doubted, but a weak voice snuck out from beneath the door.

"Mom? You can come in. I'm awake."

The 'awake' trailed off into a whisper, as though the last of her air had been spent on it, and then he heard a sucking in of breath. It was his own. He pushed the door inward and stepped through the opening to find that her bedroom had been converted to a hospital room. He followed the line from an intravenous drip down to her arm, and then followed her arm back up to her gown-clad shoulder and to her sallow face, with giant greenish-blue eyes peering through him.

"Joel?"

"Are you really better?" He couldn't stop the words from spilling out into the world. She gave him a weak smile in response.

"Sit by me?"

Joel approached the side of the bed with hesitation and then sat down on the edge, careful not to move her or touch her during the process.

"I'm not fragile," she said, her smile widening. "You can't break what's wrong with me more. Anyway, I'm better. The doctors all said they got it all in one try."

The words caressed his ears and warmed his heart, and brought tears into his troubled eyes. So it *was* true, and not everything he'd done had been a waste. Or, at least, he hadn't managed to mess up her recovery. He was brought back to reality as her fingers closed around his unsuspecting hand.

"You're crying. That's sweet," she told him.

He hadn't realized the tears had escaped. Quickly, he pulled his free hand to his face to wipe them away.

"You don't have to hide from me, Joel. I know who you are."

His mind immediately jumped back to the string of deaths with which he'd been involved, and then the never-ending parade of them that he now knew his mother had been part of. He shook his head as he rubbed his eyes, smearing tear-tracks across his cheeks.

"You don't."

"I do, Joel. I know who you are, and I know what you've been doing."

He raised his eyes slowly to come back to hers, and saw her undiluted focus was completely on him. She didn't smile anymore, only held her lips in a firm line and asked with her eyes that he believe her. Joel looked down to the floor.

"I know what that box was," Delilah whispered, her lip curling up slightly into something that resembled a smirk. Then she sucked in air and pulled her body back to make room in her lungs. It seemed to hurt her to breath, even though her operation had been for a brain tumor. She seemed to notice his inquisitive glances.

"The anesthesia has consequences, especially with my asthma. It'll pass. Don't change the subject."

"What do you think you know?" Even as the words tumbled out, the evasiveness of them made him cringe.

"I know that Franklin Thomas was killed with needle, not a knife. A needle like the one in your kit. I know he was a child molester. And I know you're a good person."

She narrowed her eyebrows, examining him for clues, but Joel tried to give none away. Still, he noticed her eyes lighten as she seemed to find something in there, something that he had failed to hide.

"I *knew* it. And Caitlynn Parker? I bet you had something to do with that one too."

He shook his head.

"I didn't," his words came out sluggish. But he knew who had ordered that. Caitlynn had been one of the most devout, good people that he'd known. Yet, just like the child molester, and the traitor, she had been marked for death at Lonnie's hand.

"Oh," she said, reading his face. She closed her eyes and for a moment Joel thought she was finished. Then she continued. "You weren't a part of killing Franklin?"

"I don't know what..."

Her face morphed into an angry glare.

"Joel, please just stop. I know. I know and I have known. I'm not an idiot."

Defeated, he dropped his head into his hands, letting the cathartic tears stream through his fingers to fall to her carpet.

"I nearly died, Joel, did you know that? While I was on the table, they killed me for about five seconds."

"I didn't want to..." Joel began, but the excuse was flimsy. He was going to say that he didn't want to kill anyone, and that was the legitimate truth. But to say that, then he would have to also explain the desperate emptiness that overrode his fear and decency to force him to do it. She wouldn't understand. "I just wanted to be closer to the Lord, Delilah. I wanted to be His tool, to work for Him. That's over now."

"Why?"

He twisted his head to see her face, catching a whiff of cleaning agents and scanning over the equipment beeping steadily next to her bed. Her face didn't mirror what he felt inside. There was no disgust lingering there, only curiosity. In fact, she hadn't seemed fazed at any point during her admission of what she knew, except when he had tried to lie. He raised an eyebrow.

"It wasn't the Lord's work," he said, stating the words for the first time out loud. "It wasn't Him."

"It was Evie."

She told him as though it were a fact instead of a question, and with more assertiveness than her deepened eye sockets and wasting body. When he looked closely, he could see that her energy was nearly depleted. She sank her head back into her pillow.

"It's so strange how little you know," she muttered, trailing off at the end. He wanted to scream at her then, and wake her up, but her mother stepped into the room so quickly that he didn't even have time to shake her.

CHAPTER 21

THE NEXT DAY, Joel made his way to the gardener's shed again. During the night and especially after speaking with Delilah, Joel knew that he was missing information. Lonnie could be one place to get it, or his mother, or apparently also Delilah, though she was too sick to inundate with questions. Joel was beginning to wonder if everyone around him knew more than he did about his own life. Even thinking of his mother filled his heart with rage as every needling comment she'd ever made surfaced at once, all while she had been sanctioning killings. The idea that he'd actually been working for her made him want to vomit. So he decided to meet with Lonnie, though from the empty shed, clearly Lonnie had not been expecting him. Joel was just walking out when Lonnie pushed his way into the room, shovel slung over his shoulder.

"Mr. Joel! I hadn't expected you back this soon."

"Who knows about what Evie and you are doing?" Mom didn't seem like the right title anymore for this woman who'd always been in love more with the church than her own child.

"Evie? Don't you mean Evie and *us*? You were there too."

"Whatever. Us. How long and who knew?"

Lonnie shrugged, tossing his shoulders back and grinning at the same time.

"You know when I arrived," he said. "That's when it became official. But before that, maybe a few years, I guess."

"*Years*? How long, exactly."

Another shrug.

"I don't know exactly, Mr. Joel. I would say before your father left, though. Maybe a year before that, I guess."

His father. Suddenly that part made a little more sense. His father must have figured it out, and left to protect himself. And left his son behind to be raised by a... monster? Joel was hardly in the position to call anyone a monster, but her involvement felt like a betrayal at the least.

"The Lord's work, Lonnie? Do you really believe in all of that?"

The question knocked the grin from Lonnie's face. He looked around the room as though he were lost for a moment, and then seemed to rally as the light came back into his eyes.

"The Lord moves in mysterious ways, Mr. Joel. I don't know if everything your mother asks is the Lord's work, but I do know that a lot of it is — like Franklin Thomas."

"And Carol Barbary?"

"Come now, Mr. Joel. Nothing happened to Carol."

"She was on the list though, wasn't she? Did that name come from Evie too?"

Lonnie nodded slowly, as though he were thinking.

"And Caitlynn Parker?"

"A mercy, Mr. Joel. She'd given all her money to the church, and the disease had barely started with her. She was going to die a slow and horrible death. The Lord's work includes mercy, remember?"

"What if she'd just kept her money instead?"

The question came from the entryway, which in his agitation, Joel had neglected to pay attention to. There, blocking the entryway and staring with cold eyes at both of them, stood Delilah, her eyes still sunken and her thin frame coated in layers of coats.

"You should be home resting," Joel said. "How did you know where to find me?"

"*You* seem to have a hard time understanding that I *know* about all of this. When you left me in the garden alone, do you think I just sat there like a castaway? I know you came to this shed and met Lonnie here, and I know what Lonnie and you have been up to. It's not as though either of you are particularly quiet. These walls are like paper."

He sucked in a breath and felt his eyes fall in their sockets.

"Then you know what monsters we are," he replied, backing away from her until his back hit a table flush with gardening supplies. Then, to his horror, he noticed Lonnie getting closer to her, step by casual step, in a way that would eventually have brought him between Delilah and the door.

"Monsters? No, I don't think so," she told them, directing her gaze toward Lonnie who stopped in his tracks. "Misguided, perhaps." She pulled at the edge of her pull-over hoodie and made to tuck her left hand back beneath the cuff.

"Misguided?"

"By Evie," she continued, her eyes never leaving Lonnie's. "Did you know that there were four people who founded this church. Before we were born, Joel, you wouldn't know. I've heard stories."

"What stories?"

"Two couples, Reynolds and Haines, wandered through the woods lost many years ago. They were on a camping trip together, exploring the Lord's wilderness, or what's left of it outside of Austin. There's still enough there to get lost in, if you watch out for the alligators or crocodiles, depending on how close you get to the ocean. Anyway, they stumbled upon a tree set at the top of a large hill. The way the sun struck from behind it concealed the small branches and leaves. From that angle, it looked just like a cross. That's when they knew that they would build a church."

"I know the founding story," Joel said. "Evie is still friends with your parents."

"You know the official version. All parties amicably agreed that your family would run the church, and the rest is history. But there's more to it than that, Joel."

She said his name, but her attention was still very much focused on Lonnie, who so far hadn't tried to approach again.

"It was the paperwork that did it. Your mother, and the Haines family, were loaded. My parents — not so much. When it came time to purchase the church grounds, your mother did it all, using cash from her trust. My parents thought it was a gesture of kindness until they realized that their names had conveniently been left off of the deed."

"It's not theirs anyway. And it's not Evie's either. This house belongs to the Lord."

Delilah smiled for the first time since entering at Joel's words.

"Joel, that's why I love you."

His heart jumped to hear her say it, and he felt its quickening pace vibrate his entire body.

"No," she said, "the truth is that the house belongs to Evie. The grounds belong to Evie. Everything here belongs to Evie, under contract. And for a while we used to all live on the church grounds. All of us, in that same house that you're in now."

He hadn't known that. His earliest memories were of his father's smile, and then it had been only he, his father, and Evie.

"Why did you move?"

"Your mother brandished the fact that we owned nothing over us every day, and eventually, to get away from her, we left the campus. But my parents still believed and believe in the church. Despite whatever she did, they believe in her. She's convincing that way."

Delilah's shoulders sunk suddenly, and Joel could tell that she was getting tired. She should have been in bed. Quickly, he pushed past Lonnie and braced her shoulders with his hands to help her stay upright. She turned and gave him a weak smile.

"Then your father left. She did the same thing to him that she did to my family. For her, she had the only vision that mattered and she needed the control to see it through. About then, like Lonnie said, is when her enemies started disappearing. I think people generally accept that people leave the church. But Joel, you have to know this. I can count on one hand the number of people who have actually left the church to have successful lives. Your father is one, and Carol Barbary is another. Once people leave the church, they tend to have short lives or bad fortunes."

Joel stole a glance at Lonnie, who now had straightened

his body as though he wasn't planning to intercept Delilah any longer, but stood shakily before them.

"Ms. Delilah, you mean that all those people..."

She nodded.

"Misguided. Just like I said. Sure, she gets it right sometimes. But mostly, she doesn't."

"Is that why your family is still here? Are they afraid of her?" Joel asked. She shook her head.

"No. They still believe in her, for some reason. They refuse to apply critical thinking to the situation. As you saw at dinner, they don't *like* her very much, but they view her as a necessary evil. You have to admit, the church has really developed under her care."

"But..." Lonnie tried to interrupt, but fell silent. Joel could feel his unease at the new information.

"But what, Lonnie?"

"All those people..."

With those words, Joel saw a different picture of Lonnie. The monster had evaporated and in its place stood a scared, lost little boy, reaching as he had for the Lord's blessing. That boy had thought that he'd found it, only to now discover that he'd been wrong, a conclusion that Joel had already long come to, but Lonnie had only now stumbled upon.

"Forget about it, Lonnie. You have a good heart, and you have tried your hardest to live by the Lord's words. You just found them in the wrong person. The Lord will forgive you."

It was in the words, or the way she said them. Even in her weakened state, the words brooked no opposition. Joel watched her eyes, still focused on Lonnie, who looked as though he might cry with his lower jaw shaking slowly. Then he surprised Joel when he dropped to his knees and prostrated himself on the floor before her.

"You are the one," he yelled, rocking and kissing the floor, sending waves of revulsion through Joel just to watch it. Joel wanted to pull the prostrating man to his feet, certain that Delilah felt the same way until he looked at her. Then he saw that her eyes still hovered over Lonnie with practiced, placid features that evoked a sense of peace. Half-closed eyelids shielded her green eyes from his inspection, and he watched as she folded her arms gently across her chest, right arm over her left wrist gripping the sleeve of her hoodie. With the green light penetrating the covered window behind, she reminded him of a painting he'd seen in the halls of the church. Mary Magdalene stared out serenely from the end of one of the halls, disciple of Jesus Christ who over-looked the entrance into the church. He averted his eyes on instinct.

"Lonnie," she said, taking a step toward the man and at the same time spiking adrenaline in Joel's brain. "You are so special. Stand up, don't do this. You are so important to me, to us, and to everything here."

Joel's mind raced as he tried to make sense of her words. He felt no fear in her, nothing matching the apprehension he felt at her unguarded words. She stood statuesque as Lonnie rose and took her hand, then resumed his kisses, one after another, until she finally pulled her hand away.

"Not now, Lonnie. Soon, I will come for you." Then she turned to leave them both, but Joel couldn't bear the thought. With a quick pace that created a warning start from Lonnie, Joel caught up to her and followed her out through the door-way. Just as they breached the entrance, she trembled, and a second later, as the door closed, she collapsed, but he caught her before she hit the ground, grabbing at her arms desper-ately as she fell.

"What was that?" He asked the question as he slowly lowered her the rest of the way, until she rested seated on the cement just outside of the gardener's door.

"What was what?" She asked. He met her eyes, and Magdalene was gone now, and she was Delilah again, his greatest source of anxiety aside from the unrelenting and uncaring Lord who he served in blindness.

"That?" He asked the question again, pointing over his shoulder to the shed.

"Oh, that. I was afraid he might kill me."

"Me too."

"I had to give him something, Joel. It was either win him over or risk being killed at his hands."

"Why come at all?"

Her eyes drew up together and the edges of her mouth slipped downward.

"No, I don't mean that. I mean, if you *knew* all of what you know, then why come? We could have talked about this in private without involving him."

"Are you less dangerous than he is?"

"No, I guess not."

She looked at him with an unflinching stare that burrowed into his mind and peeled back the surface to reveal all of his insecurities.

"I'm not dangerous to you," he said. "Never to you."

CHAPTER 22

JUST SHORT OF A WEEK LATER, it was impossible to tell that Delilah had ever been sick with the exception of her bald head, which began to recover as stubble poked its way up through her scalp. He ran his hand across the top and got it slapped away.

"That feels so weird," she giggled, as she pushed ahead of him in the church hallway. Joel walked more quickly to catch up, weaving around the parishioners who cluttered the space.

"Did they have to shave all of it?"

"You don't like it?"

"I didn't say that," he replied, taking her hand in his. "I'm only curious."

"No. They would have left a big circle in the back, though. I figured this would work out better."

She sped up, pulling him through the crowd so quickly that he stumbled to keep his feet. The entire week had gone by without a single conversation about his mother, Lonnie, the deaths, or any of it. They were only each other, and Joel forgot about the Lord's work. Nor did he feel the dread of impending death or the threat of eternal damnation lingering over his life. The constant craving for the Lord's approval had evaporated to the point that he even felt silly having obsessed about it for so long.

But that couldn't undo the wrongs he'd done.

The image of the dying man still plagued his thoughts, even though he concealed it the best he could from Delilah. Whatever she thought she knew, she'd never looked into a dying man's eyes. She'd never orchestrated the death of another, and that was something Joel knew now that he would never forget, however hard he tried.

"Skip?" she asked, as though it was even a question. He couldn't remember the last time he'd been to Bible Study. Instead, she pulled him out through the exit back out into the garden. Joel caught a glimpse of his mother's concerned eyebrows on the way through, but didn't bother talking to her, though she seemed to be trying to get his attention.

Out of the church, and through the garden, they made their way back to their usual bench, cleaned with freshly planted daisies near the base of the over-arching tree.

"My favorites," she exclaimed as she took her seat. "They're so dainty and cute."

They only looked like any other flower to him, but still he followed her suit and smiled at them, bending closer to get a whiff.

"Oh, they don't smell good," she told him as her grin widened. "Mostly like cow dung."

"Glad you told me," he replied, scrunching up his nose.

"Your mother was off of her game this morning, don't you think?" As she said the words, her smile widened even further, exposing white teeth, precursor to a possible laugh.

From his engineer's box, Joel didn't see much, and what he did see he tried to ignore.

"She was?"

Delilah nodded.

"You missed all of that stuttering? And what was up with her hair — she must not have done it this morning. Lipstick was a mess, too."

He didn't say anything, only squeezed her hand and kicked at the ground.

"You didn't see that?" She prodded him.

"Not so much. I believe you though. Do we have to talk about this?"

"No, I guess not. Just curious if you know why?"

"No reason I can think of," he lied. Lonnie hadn't talked to her in over a week, and Joel had been intentionally avoiding her as well, but Joel wanted the conversation over.

"Well, whatever it is, she deserves it," Delilah stated loudly, causing him instinctually to look around for eavesdroppers or casual observers.

"Really, what are you afraid of?" She asked him.

Again, he said nothing. The conversation was moving into a dark place, and he wanted nothing more than to be with her in peace. But he couldn't have that, it seemed.

"She's got no power anymore. Look at these," Delilah said.

She pointed again to the daisies, and Joel noticed the freshly turned up dirt underneath.

"I mentioned to Lonnie at yesterday's service that these were my favorites, and here they are. There's nothing to fear from her. She doesn't have her henchman anymore."

"How much do your parents know?"

"About?"

"About the murders. Do they know what she's been doing?"

Delilah shook her head.

"Of course not. Do you think they'd stay in the church if they did?"

"You haven't told them... all of what we talked about?"

"Why would I tell them?" As she asked the question, she reached out for his hand and grabbed it close to her chest. Then she caught his eyes with hers, and he found himself captured in her stare. "If I tell them, then they take me away from you."

"What I was thinking well..."

"What, Joel? Why is it so hard for you to talk to me?"

He shook his head and continued.

"I was thinking that maybe we could go away together. You can tell them, they can leave, that's okay. Maybe after that, you and I — I was thinking..."

The words died in his throat as he caught the dubious stare and felt her calculating eyes fall upon him. The idea hadn't so much as materialized in her subconscious at all.

"Or," she said, "we could take over the church and kick your mother out."

She followed the words with a laugh that made Joel cringe. He tried to decipher how serious she was from her tone, but her laugh bordered on incredulity and amusement, so he couldn't decide. It was only when she cut the laugh short and her eyes refocused on his that he realized she was serious. She *had* to be serious, the way she looked at him. He realized then why it mattered that Lonnie had planted her daisies, and why Joel, Evie's son, sat with Delilah on the bench in the garden instead of in Bible study.

"Not you," she said, as though she guessed his thoughts.

"You were an accident, Joel. I never meant to fall in love with you. And I am — in love with you."

"Why not leave with me then?" He pleaded. "We could leave all of this behind, and go out and find a future together."

"A future? You mean in the world beyond this campus, that your mother has worked so hard to prepare you for?"

He looked down at that, recognizing his own inadequacies. But there was one thing he was exceptional at.

"Engineering. I could do that."

"I can't leave, Joel. This is all I know."

The idea was ludicrous, and he'd known it when he said it. She would never leave if she hadn't already. Unlike him, she'd seen the corruption from the start, and guessed the rest, yet here she was, still faking her way through sermons. For a fleeting moment, he'd thought that maybe, just maybe, she might have made that choice for him. He didn't know why she couldn't leave, but he did know her reasons extended far beyond her love for him.

"What's here for you?" he asked, head swimming from confusion.

"Nothing is here for me," she told him. "Not yet."

He looked at her again, now devoid of any sign of a smile, eyes bright and focused on him alone.

"What does that mean?"

"I have a plan and if you help, we can move this church to what it *should* be."

She grabbed his hands, each one in one of hers, and pulled herself inches from his nose.

"We can do it together, Joel."

He felt the fire in her eyes drill into his and ignite something within him. His heart quickened and he felt the perspiration seep out of his forehead pores. The way she spoke, the way he couldn't look away, the way every word landed on his soul — she channeled something greater. He could *feel* it oozing off of her and seeping into him, a hot energy that made the hair on his neck stand up.

And he believed her.

"Think about it, Joel," she exclaimed, locking him down with her gaze. "No more of your mother's power-plays or games. The power in the church is in its people, not Evie. It becomes what they will it to become. The Lord doesn't care how much money you have. We need someone in charge who's less focused on the money. This prosperity gospel is a problem and the people will see through it if they're led by the right person."

"And that person is?"

She only stared at him in silence, probably waiting for him to connect the dots which, once connected, he realized was obvious.

"You?"

Her nod confirmed it as the excitement and energy, still present in her face, diminished. Then he forced a smile and nodded.

"You. You'd make the perfect choice." Another lie, and she saw through it immediately.

"You don't think I would make a great leader."

"Just...that would mean going up directly against Evie. She won't let you do it. Lonnie may be nice to you right now, but what makes you think that he'll listen to you instead if she says, oh, to *kill* you or something?"

"You think Lonnie would kill me?"

He stared into her eyes, and could see the determination of her disbelief.

"In a heartbeat," he said, then lowered his voice. "I couldn't take that."

"You're afraid of Evie?"

"Aren't you?"

"I guess you would be. She's been messing with your head since you were an infant. Look, Evie's not going to *kill* me. She's never threatened to harm anyone in our family."

"She never threatened Franklin, directly."

"But we're not child molesters, and we're not pulling members from the church. You'll see — what Evie wants, though she's doing it all wrong now, is for the church to be strong. Once she sees how much stronger the church could be with all of us working together, and not just her, she'll be all for it."

For some reason, Joel got a flash of the man he'd killed mouthing something. He struggled to see, but the image was so fleeting that he could only make out the first sound. Something that started with an 'f' — maybe 'for', or 'fur'? He couldn't figure it out before Delilah's voice came back.

"Besides, even if she did want to, why do you think I started with Lonnie first?"

And me. But that couldn't be true, though once again he went around in an uncomfortable inner dialogue about his role in all of this. By turning her own son against her, Delilah would have already sent a powerful message to the rest of the congregation. Joel was a sought-after prize, and he couldn't help the insecurity that chipped away at his back teeth.

"If she owns everything, how do you think you can get rid of her?"

"Competency clause," she stated within a beat. "The congregation can vote her out of control if they determine that she's not competent to lead."

"And you think that you have enough people, out of the millions of members that she has?"

"Oh, online members don't count in this. Only in-person attendees and congregation employees. And I've got Lonnie..."

Joel coughed loudly.

"I — I do. And I've got you," she said, pausing. "Don't I?"

"You have me," he assured her, cringing inside as he said it. "That leaves only the other two thousand to convert."

"One thousand, nine-hundred and seventy-three, precisely," she said. "But I told you, I have a plan. I just need your help."

"But Lonnie..."

Her glare stopped him, piercing through his mind and flaring up red in the back of his brain.

"Joel, stop. Don't you get it yet?"

There was no denying the edge to her voice, and the harshness of it pushed him back against the counter.

"*I'm* the dangerous one here," she told him, each syllable clipped at the end. A cold shiver worked its way through his body as he realized that he believed her. Then she smiled and shook it off. "Pretty convincing, right? So let's get down to the plan."

For a formerly dying person, her energy seemed to spike when she discussed her plan, especially when she outlined his role in it. He (and she) would both start attending Bible Study and working on people there, whatever that meant. She told him that it just meant being nice to people, even if they had to fake it. Joel was well-practiced at faking many things so the chore wouldn't be too difficult. She would handle the rest.

All the while she talked, the image of her fixed jaw and

unforgiving stare when she'd denounced Evie as a threat stuck in his head, overlapping her gestures and pronunciations. All he could hear were her words: "I'm the dangerous one here". The flip had happened so quickly that he found himself looking for aspects of that face she'd made in every one of her motions, but it couldn't be found. The animated person she was now, laying out the strategy for her coup, wasn't the same person he'd witnessed before. Rather, it was, but almost like a veneer had been stapled over her face. Or was the former the veneer, as she'd informed him? There was no way to know, and part of him, a big part that was now in control and craved her attention and affection, even while recognizing it as a substitute for the Lord's light — that part of him didn't want to know. That part of him smiled and nodded as she talked, and held her hand tightly, swinging from every word.

Another part of him wondered instead about the Lord. Would he ever feel the warm glow of the Lord's love? He'd hurt people. So many people. He questioned now, in spite of the evidence of Delilah's recovery, and despite his desire to *believe and belong*, whether he'd ever done the Lord's work at all. Had Joel only participated in his mother's shrewd calculations to keep the church strong?

A smaller and meeker part of him already suspected the answer was yes.

CHAPTER 23

THE NEXT DAY WAS SUNDAY, and Delilah's plan had been under way for all of half an hour while Bible study was in progress. As it turned out, Joel didn't have to initiate much. Every time the circle leader called for a break, people came up to Joel and asked him questions about him and Delilah. The first was the Parker boy, who seemed skittish at first.

"Joel?" He asked, dark hair covering his eyes and looming over Joel's head. "I heard you disagreed with what your mother said to my mom about her giving all of our money to the church. Someone said that you got into a fight with her about it. Is that true?"

Joel spared a glance for Delilah who sat just across from him and only smiled.

"I guess," he said. "How did you come to hear about that?"

To his knowledge, nobody had been in the room. And his disagreement had been less an argument than a pout, but still, that seemed to matter to Greg Parker, who shoved his hair out of the way revealing his bespectacled face. From the angle, Joel couldn't make out his eyes past the high-glare reflection of the light overhead, but as he bent forward, Joel could see tears in the corners of his eyes.

"I know you couldn't stop what happened," he whispered. "Thank you so much though. You stood up for her when she couldn't do it for herself. Even if she didn't listen, I know she knew how much you cared. I'll never forget that."

Joel felt his own eyes misting over, and he ran his hand across his face quickly to mask the tears and steal them before they fell.

"I didn't do anything," he said, letting the words stand out in the air. Greg looked confused for a minute, and then he smiled, shaking his head side-to-side.

"I won't mention it again," Greg said. "I just wanted to tell you that, you know, if anything should happen, me and the rest of my family — we appreciate what you've done for us, and we won't forget."

Before Joel could protest further, Greg backed away and found his seat, Joel's eyes following him as he did, then skipping over to Delilah, who met his gaze. She smiled a thin, secretive smile that disappeared almost as quickly as it arrived, and another person nudged his shoulder. This one was David, Greg's best friend who had challenged Joel over his mom's part in Mrs. Parker's death the day after she'd died.

"Joel, you decided to come back to Bible study." He clapped Joel on the back as if they were friends, but Joel only squirmed under his touch. "I heard you and Delilah are dating now. Well done! And way to keep it to the church royalty."

"Not sure what that means, David."

"Just that we know where the power is, and we've got

your back. That harpy of a mother of yours can't keep you down forever."

Joel turned the words over in his mind. He felt his breath stop as he considered the interactions — two in less than five minutes, both about his tenuous relationship between he and his mother. Had the frayed threads of their relationship been so obviously visible? No. He was certain that until that morning, he'd been careful to play the dutiful son. One more glance at Delilah answered his question, as she met his eyes with a twinkle and a wave.

"What have you been telling them?" He asked in a hoarse whisper as she left the room. "What does everyone think is going on?"

"I haven't told them anything that wasn't true. Greg came to visit me when I was sick, so I may have let it slip that your mother was controlling you and trying to keep us apart. Then he opened up about his own mother. Did you know that she had her doubts about giving everything to the church? She prayed on that for days before finally deciding to give all of her money, including Greg's college fund, to the church. And for what? She died and now they're broke."

"Why do they still come?"

She shrugged as she took his hand and guided him down the hallway with her.

"Loss, I guess. Greg's father hasn't been the same since she died. He was in a downward spiral, and for a while hated the church and everyone in it. But then, I guess he found religion again, and now he's more dedicated than ever."

"And David?"

"Oh, that. He's always hated your mother, and frankly Joel, until last week, they all kind of thought you were blind to her manipulations."

He stopped hard, pulling himself out of the flow of traffic and her with him.

"I was never blind to it," he told her, careful to guard his expressions now that he was aware that so many eyes were watching. "You all don't understand what it's like to be the heir apparent to this monstrous thing, and not even be able to feel the Lord's love in you."

He snapped his mouth shut and awaited her judgment. Her eyes scanned over his face, following the edge of his wide eyes as he felt the tears forming in his lower lids, tears that he blinked away rapidly. She followed the contours of his jaw and the ridge of his nose as though she were looking for something, seeking some evidence supporting his words. Then she pulled closer to him.

"We can't talk about this here" She whispered as she turned to glance over her shoulder. "Let's go."

A moment later, she pulled him out of the hallway, only instead of moving toward their normal pavilion as he'd expected, she walked briskly toward the edge of the complex. It took him a moment to realize that they were moving in the direction of her home. Once they'd cleared the majority of the foot traffic flowing toward the parking lot, she slowed her pace and smiled, staring straight ahead.

Joel followed obediently, feeling ice forming on his innards and somehow his heart beating rapidly, but never fast enough to heat the frost inside. He shivered at the thought of his exposure, that in a moment of weakness he'd finally revealed his hidden truth. The Lord had never seen fit, through everything in his life, to make his presence known to Joel. All of Joel's sacrifices had come to naught. He felt himself shrinking into a ball, and then smaller as the ball crumpled into nothing. Her voice brought him out of it.

"You never told me that before. That's probably the most personal thing that you've ever shared with me," she said. "Thank you."

He gulped and for a moment didn't respond, not having a response to offer. Even at that moment, the most powerful feeling he could identify was the longing to be in her presence, and the crippling fear that every word he spoke would somehow force a wedge between them, something he couldn't lose. This feeling was the closest thing that he had ever felt to what he imagined the Lord's love would be like.

"Joel, did you hear me?"

"I heard."

"Thank you. That's sweet that you're finally starting to trust me enough to let me in. Can I share a secret with you as well?"

He nodded.

"That group in there," she said, "half of them can't feel it either. They're all faking it like you are. The other half are probably borderline crazy."

He blinked.

"But *you* feel the Lord's love, right?"

"No, not directly. That's not what faith is, Joel. How easy would it be if His love was *that* obvious that people could actually feel it with any real comprehension. I'd guess that Lonnie is probably the only one I've met who feels the Lord with any certainty, and he's obviously got it wrong."

His head spun at that. He'd never considered how others interacted with the Lord, or at least, hadn't beyond the speaking in tongues and the prayers and hymns. Was she right?

"My mother..."

"Maybe, possibly, your mother feels something. That's

probably true, I guess. I know my parents do. But they're wrong, and your mother's wrong. You really thought that we're all swimming in the Lord's favor or something? It doesn't work that way."

"How does it work then?"

"That's what I've been trying to tell you. That feeling isn't something that just comes. It's faith, and prayer, and dedication, and nurturing a *personal* relationship with the Lord. This stuff about how many cars you own or how much you can afford to give to the church? It's all bullshit. That's what I want to change."

CHAPTER 24

BIBLE STUDY CHANGED after that Saturday. Every lecture topic seemed designed to chastise them, dipping into the books of Romans, Timothy, and Paul to push authority and obedience to authority. Joel could feel Evie's hand in the mix. She outlined the courses for Bible study each year, and this shift in focus to obedience wasn't at all consistent with the message of brotherly love from before. Others seemed to feel it too as more and more of them gathered after church.

Delilah and Joel's tree turned into an informal gathering place, where they met to air grievances and plan out what to do next. A group of students skipped Bible study to join them and listen to them talk. As the group grew over the next few weeks, Joel was surprised to see that Lonnie attended as well. At first, the man, conspicuous against the backdrop of children from Bible study, lingered near the walkway and the students gave him wide berth. It took a month, but eventually he became just one of the growing pack.

Not everyone in Bible study came to their clandestine meetings. Those who didn't seemed to withdraw from

Delilah and Joel, and barely made eye contact with them. In the circle, they occupied one side, while Delilah's group occupied the other. And, when the instructor began to lecture about obedience and discipline and respect for authority, members in that group seemed to come alive with support.

"Evie's brood." Delilah dubbed them one day after Bible study, as she and Joel made their way to their bench, half of the classroom in tow. That name stuck, and every Bible study after, Joel heard the whispers "Evie's brood" slink through the classroom. That was all it took to silence the others, and eventually, the only voices responding to the teachings were in dissent.

"Why are you fighting the Lord's word?" The instructor pleaded with the class, trying to regain control. Nobody answered, and most of the class looked toward Delilah to answer.

"Nobody's fighting against the Lord's word," she replied. "We're fighting *for* it. You can't take those passages out of context. Paul says to respect your parents and the government that you live in, but he also says that the government should represent the will of the Lord. You keep leaving that part out."

Abashed by her comments, the instructor opened his mouth, then shut it again.

"And Timothy said the same thing," she continued. "He said that the authority must follow the Lord. It's not only the lay people who are accountable, but also the authorities themselves."

"You think it's easy to get up here every week and try to teach you? This is hard, and there's not time to get into the nuance of every little thing. We'll cover that later."

"By then, the damage is done. We need to know the whole story *now*, not later."

"I've had it."

The instructor, one of the many volunteers who helped the church function, dropped his copy of the Bible into his bag and stormed from the room, leaving the group to whisper amongst themselves.

"What do we do now?" Someone whispered.

"Delilah can teach us," another voice said, and then another agreed. Within moments, more than half of the room urged her to teach them. As soon as she nodded and stood in the circle as the instructor had done, four of the remaining students grabbed their bags and headed toward the door after the old circle leader. David stepped between them and the exit, causing a frantic pushing but they couldn't move him.

"Let them," commanded Delilah, and immediately David moved aside, and the four others pushed in a tight cluster through the doorway into the hall. Watching all of this, Joel felt sick to his stomach. The feeling had begun that first day after the surgery, but over the course of the weeks, it had only gotten worse. He clenched his teeth to keep the feeling at bay.

"Where were we?" she asked, looking around the room, making eye contact with each person in turn. Her hair had grown back to almost an inch, so that it lay down now at least, except for on the sides where it still poked out, making her head look like it was on fire.

"Ah yes," she said, as her eyes fell on Joel. "Civil disobedience in the Bible. How about some new reading? Samuel 1, verse 14:45, when the Lord commanded the people of Israel to not harm a hair on Jonathon's head under the corruption of King Saul."

Joel felt the muscles in his abdomen contract as the feeling in his gut intensified.

———

A teacup the size of a house broke through the clouds and settled slowly toward the earth. If it wasn't for the obviously excessive altitude, Joel might have mistaken the teacup — not a real teacup but a volantrae that somewhat resembled one — for a designer vehicle. That would have contradicted his dream state confidence that this was in fact a teacup and that the occupants were aliens. As the vehicle descended in an ocean of conspicuous silence, he could only stare in awe until it settled on its saucer-like base and a thin doorway opened in the side. Out popped the first alien he'd ever seen in his entire life.

This alien took the form of a tall raven-haired woman in a teal sari, though in the confidence that comes with dreams, Joel knew that she was an alien. She disembarked and stepped gracefully through the opening before she placed her feet onto the soft earth, the points of her short heels digging into the ground.

"Joel," she told him, opening her arms as though she had known him forever and expected a hug. His reaction, stemmed by revulsion at her alienness, was to cower away.

"It's me Joel. The Lord. I'm who you've been looking for."

Joel squinted at the woman, whose sari now began to billow toward him as a rogue wind escaped from the ships hatch.

"Who are you?"

"The Lord, Joel. You've been doing work for me, remember?"

Over her shoulder, a cluster of heads appeared. Although he couldn't make out the bodies or the people in their entirety, he knew that Franklin would be among them, and the others he'd witnessed murdered, and murdered himself.

"These were mine, Joel. I received your paeans and they pleased me, so I came to see you."

The coincidences had mounted too quickly, so Joel knew this had to be the Lord. He stepped forward, only now noticing his bare feet, which he followed up to his bare calves and bare thighs. By the chill that followed, he knew now that he was completely naked, and drew his hands around his privates to offer some cover.

"Don't be silly, Joel. I'm the Lord, remember?"

"You can't be."

"Now you understand, don't you? If you refuse to see me as the Lord, how can you feel me when I talk to you? You say you want to believe, but you won't believe, will you?"

Joel felt tears forming in his eyes and snorted as he tried vainly to keep his nose from running as well. He failed to keep either the tears or the mucus constrained.

"I *do* believe. You're an alien. Your ship is right there."

He hazarded some privacy to point to her teacup, which was already beginning to lift back off of the ground. She didn't look as he pointed, jabbing his finger behind her repeatedly. While he did so, she began to blur. In his peripheral vision, her hair shortened and changed colors lightening from black to dark brown and then finally morphing into a red boy-cut. He knew what he would see if he shifted his gaze back to her, and at first he resisted. No matter what forms this alien took, he knew that she wasn't the Lord.

But when his eyes betrayed him and locked on the woman before him, she was no longer wearing a teal sari at all, and the people behind her as well as the teacup disappeared up into the sky. It was only her, Delilah, as naked as he was, standing alone before him in a deep field of grass and flowers.

"It's me, Joel. Why don't you know me?"

"You can't be the Lord. You can't be..."

"Joel, it's me. Joel, why can't you feel me?"

In a bout of frustration, he wiped stinging tears from his eyes. "None of this is real," he told himself. "It's only a dream."

Then she sucked in a deep breath.

"Joel!" She screamed so loudly that he felt his head vibrate with the after effects.

"No, it can't be you."

The voice came again, but this time it didn't sound right. It hollowed out and took on a husky quality, like someone much older.

"Joel! Open the door!"

Confused, he looked around him for a door to open, but there was no door. He looked back at her, and noticed that her lips no longer moved with the sound. The scream came from somewhere else. She seemed to realize it too and began to move quickly toward him, her arms at first pinned by her sides and then one arm draped across her torso and her other arm reaching toward him. Without thinking, he ran toward her too, feeling an ending looming, when the voice came again.

"Open the door!"

———

Joel awoke to his heart pounding and sweat beading already on his forehead. The room had grown so cold that his breath pushed out little clouds of steam before him.

"Open the door, Joel. We need to talk."

Now that he heard the voice again, it sounded like his mother. Still reeling from the dream, he twisted himself out of bed and made his way to his locked door, pausing before it. He had managed to avoid his mother for several weeks, taking his meals after she'd gone to bed, and only doing the requisite troubleshooting and preparation for each of the events. He sighed and reached out for the handle before realizing that he had a lingering erection from the dream. Scrambling, he grabbed his blanket and threw it over his shoulders, then twisted the doorknob, only to have his mother push past him into the room.

"You know what they're saying about me?" She asked him the question, and he paused for thirty seconds before deciding that it wasn't a question that warranted a response. In that short time, he took in her appearance. Her black hair was disheveled and he could tell her extensions hadn't been added yet. Her wide eyes sported red tendrils like spokes around her irises. Her thin white tee-shirt hung from her shoulders.

"N-no," he answered.

"I'm not fit to lead the church," she said, taking a moment to glare at him as though she knew his answer wasn't true. Still he maintained innocence.

"So what?" He asked. "*You* know you're fit to lead, right?"

"Do you believe that?"

The words hung in the air between them and all he could think about was Delilah, her imagined body bouncing through the tall grass, struggling to reach him and him failing and that split-second that he awoke, longing for a moment he could never retrieve, one that he wished with futility to reconstruct, but inevitably impossible. He thought about her and about Lonnie and about Delilah and her illness. In that same second he thought of Franklin and Greg and Carol and the rest. All of the chaos and destruction had happened under her watch, and most originated with her, so he couldn't tell her honestly that he thought she was fit to lead. His impulse to lie was shattered by the single fact that she was his mother. Instead, he said nothing.

"You don't?" She made the statement as though it were a question, but again he knew better than to respond. "Why do you think I *do* all of this, Joel? Do you think I *like* what I've become? Do you seriously believe that when I founded this church, I thought that I would be killing people I care about?"

"Of course not," he finally responded, "but you never had to end up here. You could have just let things go. Carol, Caitlyn, Franklin, and others. What's the worst that could really happen if you did *nothing*?"

The look on her face told him everything he needed to know. The possibility of not interfering in the lives of others — in persuading them instead of eliminating her competition — had never really entered her mind. In that moment, her face changed, eyes shifting downward and the corners of her lips turning downward.

"Joel," she told him, "it's always been about you, you know?"

He shook his head, though he wanted to believe her. The idea that she built her future around him was tantalizing, but that couldn't have been the truth. Not after what Delilah had revealed.

"No, Evie. That's not what happened. You consolidated power from the moment you established the church." He realized as he finished that his voice had risen and that he had practically shouted the last three words.

"I didn't. I tried hard to make it work. You weren't there."

"So you didn't put this entire building, the entire *campus*, in your own name? You didn't lord that over Delilah's parents, my *father*? None of that is true?"

She shifted her approach and lowered her voice.

"They never liked me," she told him. "Even from the very beginning. They didn't like me and I worshipped your father. I mean it. I lived or died by that man. It was *his* idea to keep the ownership between he and I and leave the Reynolds's out. Your wonderful father. *Not* me."

"How could I know? You never let me talk to him."

"What? Ridiculous. You have your own communicator there in your drawer. I gave it to you when you were eight. *I* never stopped you from talking to your father. *You* decided you didn't want to talk to him anymore."

As she said the words, the moment came back to him. Angry and bitter at the fact that his father had never actually called him, Joel decided that this revenge would be the same. Never call his father, and for several years after his eighth birthday, he didn't. He remembered now, but that didn't excuse the rest.

"What about the rest?"

"True enough, Joel. Like I said, that was for you. You have to understand! I have no skills. None. I can't even make bread. The only thing I can do reasonably well is take care of this church. And I do that so that *you* have a chance in this life. It's cruel out there, and I really hope that you never have to understand how incredibly cruel it is. I did what I had to do."

"And we're doing what we have to do."

Those words, ushered from his own mouth of his own impossible volition, crippled her down to the earth. She didn't respond.

"There's a better way, Evie. The Lord doesn't care how much people make. The Lord is uninterested in money at all. The Lord only cares about how we look out for each other and ourselves. Delilah knows this. Why can't you see it?"

"That's a beautiful sentiment, son. But what happens when only poor people come to the Lord's house?"

She moved toward him, shuffling her feet. Self-conscious, he didn't move a muscle from where he stood, and clutched the blanket more tightly around his body, stiffening his muscles involuntarily. Evie seemed to notice this and stopped almost a foot away from him. She cocked her head sideways and looked at him.

"This is what I have to offer, Joel. And it's all I have to give you."

Her hands both went up at the same time, fingers skyward.

"This church is your inheritance. A Haines started it, and your father and I wanted to have something to leave you when we die."

"Delilah told me what you did, Evie. She told me about running my father off."

Her hands fell to her side.

"What did that bitch tell you?!"

She clasped her hand to her mouth as the words escaped between her fingers. Then she clenched her teeth and pulled her hand away. Her fingers danced around her throat as she continued.

"Your *father* didn't leave because of me. He found what he wanted in some slinky young thing that attended the Bible service and ran off to fuck her with half of the church's money. Is *that* what she told you?"

"N-not exactly the same story," he muttered, now ready to let the blanket fall, and grateful when it did and let in a cool blast of air to offset the flush he felt in his skin.

"He ran off with one of the early parishioners, I think her name was Tina. I don't know if he was ever here for the church or if he was drawn to the power, Joel. I know what you and your girl are playing at, and you'll find out soon. Some people in our congregation are here for the Church, some for the Lord, and some for the Power. You can guess which your little bitch is here for."

"She's not a bitch, Evie. Stop calling her names. She may have gotten the story wrong, but not the whole story? You and her parents founded this church, and you cut them out."

His mother searched the room for a place to sit, which she found beneath a pile of clothes in his only chair. She dumped them to the floor and collapsed into it, then turned her head back to him.

"No, I guess she's not a bitch," Evie said, her eyes filled with tears. "But what would you want me to call the woman turning my own son against me."

He sucked in air through clenched teeth and furrowed his eyebrows.

"You really are something, Evie."

"I'm your mother. Stop calling me Evie. I hate that you started doing that."

"Evie," he persisted, "listen. It's my turn. You don't seem

to understand the situation. I've *killed* people — people that *you* asked to be killed. I was your assassin. What do you think that does to us?"

"But *why*, beloved? I asked you not to get too close to Lonnie, and you did it anyway. I asked Lonnie to leave you alone, and he did the opposite. So I stopped interfering, hoping in my heart that I put enough of the Lord in you to guide you."

"And you didn't," he finished. "There's no Lord in me, mother."

He said the words while recalling his dream. Delilah's voice bounced through his head. 'I am the Lord. Why won't you see me?' He gulped quietly. "There never has been any Lord in me. I can't *feel* him, Mom. I can't feel the Lord and I've been in this church watching people get saved for my entire life."

"You never talked to me about it Joel. You never..."

"Acting like you care now won't change anything. You never had time for me, or when you did, it was for grooming me to look the right way. This entire thing is just a performance. I don't know what *you* think it is — maybe you feel something in there somewhere."

"What do you know about it," she spat, the words filled with venom. "You've never had to struggle in your entire life. Maybe that's what made you so soft and pliable." By the end, her harshness had evaporated into nothing, and he could see her shoulders slumping. She slowly rose to her feet, tears now on full display, and he'd never noticed her so weak before. Shuffling toward the door, she cleared her throat.

"This was all for you, Joel. I know you'll never believe it, but it was."

Then she left.

CHAPTER 25

SERVICE PASSED the next Saturday without a single look from his mother, who arrived on time and as prepared as ever. She delivered a flawless sermon, and then the groups broke out for Bible study. The Bible study instructor showed up again, looking sheepish with downcast eyes, but Delilah didn't yield the floor. The four who had defended him the day before skipped the meeting so it turned into a conversation about the direction of the church for the entire hour. As the conversation went on, even the instructor, seated amongst the students, posed questions directed to Delilah seeking guidance.

Joel had suspicions about that. He guessed that the Bible study instructor's lessons had been chosen explicitly by Evie to quell any unrest, and that the instructor, as devout and committed as he was to the church and to Evie, had decided during the evening that selective teaching wasn't really teaching and that Delilah had been right to challenge him. Delilah had that effect on people — they generally wanted to make her happy. Joel listened form the back as she rattled on about loyalty and building a personal relationship with the Lord, not once saying anything linking prosperity on earth to the Lord.

As she gave her sermon, countering much of Evie's from earlier that day, Joel only heard one phrase.

Why won't you see me?

He explored his feelings about Delilah, his longing, his affection, and her commitment to his happiness and returned affection for him. His eyes locked on her, with her hands flowing through the air as she explained how the Lord worked to save people, and how He reached into the hearts of each and every person, and for the first time, Joel believed that to be true. Joel felt warmth spread through his chest and abdomen as he watched her boy-cut framed eyes express a contagious excitement that sparked like electricity through the small crowd. She spoke so loudly that others passing in the hall outside poked their heads in as well, some pushing in to stay and hear what this flaming-haired girl had to discuss.

A natural vessel for the Lord. The thought originated from somewhere deep within Joel's consciousness and took hold. The feelings he had must have been the sparking of his Lord's fire within, and now he finally had something that he could call the Lord to love. He smiled a wide grin and she ever so slightly returned it with her eyes.

———

The house felt empty when he awoke on Sunday, and only the air purification unit marred the serene garden soundscape. Joel made his way to the kitchen, turning each corner with his imagination first, then his eyes, as he moved quickly to avoid any potential collision. His mother, Evie, had to be there somewhere, running through her morning sermon. It would be similar to yesterday's, which he'd been impressed with as she ran through it without a flaw. He hadn't even had to tweak the simulcast as she'd stayed in front of the camera, and on the appropriate platform, the entire time. He hadn't thought about it the day of, but that part was strange. Usually she teased the edges of the cameras, getting as close as she could to the crowd who had come to learn about the Lord.

She wasn't in the hallway that joined his room to the kitchen, where he made some quick toast before he made his silent escape, preferring to spend mornings in the garden instead of in the house where difficult conversation may be thrust upon him at any moment. If he had to listen to one more lecture about how dumb he was being, and how Delilah was the devil, and how much Evie loved him, even now as he betrayed her...it got old. Instead, he preferred to walk among the flowers and plants, and feel the remaining chill in the Texas air dissipate as the sun breached the horizon and brought its unrelenting rays down across the state.

When the fiery orb reached the top of the poplar trees, Joel knew that it was time for sermon, or nearly time, from where he was lost in the garden. Approaching the church parking from the periphery, walking around an outcrop of trees almost into the street, Joel saw the intermixed cars and volantrae occupying the various slots. A shoebox-shaped volantrae lowered just above his head and took a space before him as he walked, causing him to turn slightly and make his way around the vehicle. Just beyond, on the sidewalk, a crowd of older men stood, none of them aware that he was there until he breached the edge of the walkway. Then three of the four of them looked his direction at the same time. One of them recognized him and raised his hand in a friendly wave, accompanied by a toothy smile. Joel smiled back, automatically returning the surface-deep gesture while at the same time examining the crowd beyond them for one of three people: Evie, Delilah, or Lonnie. None of the three could be found.

Half an hour later, churning through several more uncomfortable greetings, Joel made his way to the engineer booth, and flipped on the controls to start the day. He'd missed checking the controls, but had done so little the day before that he couldn't imagine any problems. He warmed up the board with a quick switch, then spun a knob that engaged the stage spotlight, half expecting to see Evie had beaten him to the stage — but she wasn't there. A gnawing feeling chewed at the back of his throat as his eyes once again walked the edges of the crowd, but against the formal saris and sherwanis that the older folks wore, replete with golds, silvers, reds, and rich blues, he couldn't find his mother in her traditional pantsuit. His eyes came to a rest and he realized that the spot that he focused on wasn't the stage any longer, but where Delilah used to stand in the audience just before it. He looked again for Delilah's straight short hair and her bobbing head. He couldn't find her either. With another switch, he piped the music in, his mother's cue to come out on stage. Again his mother failed to present.

As he was about to rise to check on her, he saw Delilah, and his eyes wouldn't leave her. They followed her through the crowd as the groups raucous sounds diminished into whispers in her wake. The forest green salwar kameez styled gown with gold trim that she wore advertised the fact that she must have been feeling better. It was a style typically worn by the adults in the church, not children, as he somehow still considered himself and Delilah both, despite the waves they made. Completing the outfit, an emerald suspended from her red hair just between her eyes that made them pop almost like fluorescents. Nobody seemed to notice the empty stage as she approached.

Joel noticed additional movement near the back entrance. He willed his eyes toward the action and saw Lonnie closing the door just behind the crowd, ducking behind some people as he entered. He seemed winded and flustered, but then he always seemed that way, so Joel paid no mind. His attention swung back to Delilah to once again feel the peace that she projected even more with her manner, as people seemed to drift out of her path, guiding her toward her normal position near the stage, a kindness never offered to anyone in the crowd's urgency to learn more of the Lord's story. Yet this time, they made an exception.

And still no Evie. This had *never* happened in his entire existence at the church. When Delilah settled into her place, the sounds from the crowd seemed to rise again into the roar of a river, only to die shortly after into an animal's whimper as everyone turned their attention to the stage. Joel then remembered that he hadn't yet enabled the broadcast, so he flipped the knob to prime the multicast and tried to duck back out of sight. He couldn't completely hide in the engineer booth, but he could cover most of his body behind the high walls. As he did, he noticed that the eyes which had a moment before been focused on the stage had all swiveled to him, as though he was the de-facto stand-in now that his mother didn't seem to be present.

He debated going back to their living quarters to try to find her. It was possible she overslept, he considered, though that would be unusual. She'd never done so before. Instead, not entirely sure why, he rose, and the eyes rose with him. Then he cut across the stage, taking the stairs from his booth and crossing to the platform where his mother usually stood. His heart pounded against his ribcage and each step felt as though he walked through a thick, sucking mud as he made his way. Because of the acoustical design, there was no need for a microphone once he arrived. Every sound, even the sound of his elevated breathing, projected out over the crowd and now, through the simulcast as well.

"I'm afraid we'll have to postpone service today," he told the crowd, not knowing what else to do in his mother's absence. The crowd disagreed, as murmurs of dissent flitted through. He felt the perspiration gathering against his forehead and he ran his fingers through his thick black curls,

"My mother — Evie — she's not here. I'll have to..."

Before he could continue, he saw more movement from the group. Delilah made her way toward him, taking the stairs normally reserved for miracle healings or prayer requests. The crowd's sounds died out as she captured their attention and made her way toward Joel, her eyes locked on him, and her mouth moving, saying something he couldn't quite make out with the stage lighting. He squinted toward her, but it was no good. Only when she finally approached his podium could he make out the words.

"Don't," she was saying. Then a second later, "Introduce me."

Grateful for any opportunity to exit the scrutiny of the crowds, he nodded.

"Ladies and gentlemen, we'll be having a guest speaker today. Ms. Delilah Reynolds." As he finished, he reached out with a hand to grab hers and help pull her onto the podium. Murmurs again flowed like ocean waves through the crowd.

Somewhere in the back, someone clapped unrelentingly and that seemed to seed the crowd as applause rose. The sounds of disquiet were quickly drowned out by the cheers and screams of delight.

Joel left her up there, disappearing as quickly as he could back into the safe invisibility of the engineer booth, while Delilah, looking as comfortable and unintimidated as she always did, raised a jeweled hand to quiet the crowd.

"When's the last time you thought about your personal relationship with the Lord?" She asked the question to a confused audience, one who may not have been prepared for it. They looked at each other at first, trading incredulous glances, but she seemed not to notice.

"We've been teaching a lot about what rewards the Lord will give in this life to those who do his will, and maybe, to some extent, there's some truth there. But who among you really *know* that your relationship with the Lord is what it needs to be? Or... are you going through the motions?"

That last question seemed to stifle the crowd. Naysayers preoccupied themselves with examining each other for defects and tried to avert their eyes, but few succeeded. The way she looked at everyone, fearless and determined, she was impossible to resist. She stared as though she looked through people and into their lives, reading their entire histories. He'd never seen her use that look on him, but she used it unrelentingly against those in the crowd who muttered in dissatisfaction. With cold dispassion, her gaze followed the sounds of dissent, and everywhere her eyes landed, silence followed, because *she* seemed to have the power to lay out their secrets.

As the sermon continued, Joel watched Lonnie work his way toward the front. Unlike Delilah, for whom the crowd had parted in awe, they parted for him in fear. Even though as far as he knew, nobody else there was aware of his role as the church enforcer, the crowd seemed to sense the danger in him, and the sea split before him in frantic bursts, revealing openings that closed only after he'd passed several rows. Then, Lonnie was back in his usual place, gyrating to the music, tears streaming down his face.

The tears caught Joel's mind. He had seen tears before at the funeral of Lonnie's victims, as the man prostrated himself against the coffin. Joel's mind retraced his steps back to the beginning of Delilah's sermon, when both Delilah and Lonnie had arrived at the exact same time Joel had discovered his mother missing. Joel's stomach suddenly felt ill and he slid down into his seat, chastising himself for an overactive imagination. After the sermon, he would search their living quarters and find his mother had slept in, overworked and overstressed and finally succumbing to being an actual human. It would almost be a relief to find that at one time in her life, she did have weaknesses, and even he being among those weaknesses meant that she did love him, in a strange way. He would find her, and everything would be fine, and the next weekend, everything would be back to normal.

That was it exactly. His stomach recovered enough for him to realize that Delilah had moved to the edge of the simulcast viewing area and he quickly adjusted the count, noticing the numbers across his dashboard. The simulcast had already blown past a million and neared two, numbers flipping five per second. He looked again, mouth hanging open, as they ticked past three. Then he heard a yell from someone in the audience nearby.

"The news! We made the news!"

Everything before him was used for projecting out and not for monitoring virtual reality or other two-way communication, so he craned forward out of the box looking into the crowd.

"What?" He demanded in a harsh whisper to see. The person who had yelled held up what looked like a tablet, but small enough to fit into a hand, and flipped it around to show Joel. Sure enough, the morning news had tapped into the simulcast and the words across the screen read "Is this dazzling new face a sign of change in the Austin Life Community Church?". There above the words he could make out Delilah's features in a captured still.

————

Joel skipped Bible study alone for the first time since he'd begun to associate with Delilah. He burst through the door to his and his mother's shared living quarters that he'd often called home. Straight back was the kitchen, and at a glance, he could tell that nothing there had been disturbed since he left. Taking a deep lung of air, Joel made his way past the kitchen and down a narrow hallway toward the room in which his mother slept. He bit his lip when he knocked, as afraid of gaining her attention as he was of there being no response whatsoever. Each knock rang out and echoed in silence, impotent in attracting any response. With a nudge, he forced the door open, which didn't take much effort as it was unlocked.

The bed was still made, and he doubted that it had been slept in. Otherwise, the room was completely empty and everything, true to his mother's nature, was in precisely the place he would have expected.

He turned back through the doorway and made his way back to the kitchen, taking a closer look at the oven. It still held the crumbs from his morning toast, something his anal-retentive mother wouldn't have left uncleaned.

A knock sounded in the room. Without thinking, he sprinted across toward the door and flung it open as wide as it would go. Expecting his mother, instead he was presented with a mixture of dark green and gold.

"It's you," he muttered, and turned to examine the living quarters once more, but there was no point. Their quarters were tiny compared to the complex on which they lived. Evie wasn't there, nor had she been there since he left. "Shouldn't you be in Bible study?"

"Not when your mother is missing, Joel," she responded with an edge to her voice. "I came to see if she was here. Is she in there?"

"No," he shrugged. "I'm not even sure she came home last night."

"You don't think she did?"

"Nothing's moved at all except for what I did this morning. She wasn't here."

"Any idea where she might be?"

"No," he said offhand. But then he remembered Caitlyn Parker prostrating herself in the pastor's office. "Maybe." Joel turned and pushed past Delilah out into the hallway at a quick walk, resisting the urge to run and with Delilah close behind. They shot out through the door to the house and back toward the main campus. Inside, Joel followed a lengthy hallway that ran back toward the main gathering chamber, and then past that toward a tiny cluster of offices including the pastor's office that his mother often spent time in. His mother was not to be found in any of the rooms or hallways they checked.

"Where could she be?" he asked, forgetting for a moment

that Delilah was there with him, and not expecting an answer. He jumped when Delilah broke her silence.

"Anywhere she wants, I suppose. She's a grown woman after all."

"No, she'd never leave the church unguarded."

"You're here."

"Not even with me here. There's just no way she'd do that."

"She's not even missing, Joel. With all that's going on, maybe she just needed some space. Don't we all feel that way sometimes?"

"I know you may not want to find her, but I do!" he snapped at her, and immediately regretted his outburst. "I didn't mean to scream at you."

"I know," she told him, grasping his fingers between hers. "I *know*. Just trust that the Lord will look after her. She probably did need some time to herself."

"Yeah," he said, glancing around the room one more time. "Yeah, you're probably right."

With that, he turned to leave, her following after him, leaving the office as empty as he'd found it.

CHAPTER 26

AFTER TWO DAYS and no mother, Joel wanted to call the local police. He stared at his communicator, sitting unused on his desk across from the bed. Every time he worked up the nerve to use the device, he remembered the woman in the teal sari, just before changing into Delilah, who told him with her straight black hair blowing in the wind, that he had done the Lord's work. He *had* been doing work, the Lord's or not, which the police would be very interested in knowing about. Who knew what else they might uncover while investigating his mother's absence. His mother, who as Delilah reminded him frequently, could also just be sojourning somewhere.

"Penny for your thoughts?" Delilah had been practically tied to his side for the previous few days, going as far as spending the evenings on the couch in the living room. Now, though, she played a game on her tablet beside him on his bed. His kit lay open on the desk before him and even with its ominous presence there, and her beside him, he felt no shame in it any longer. After all, *she* hadn't found any shame in it at all, and had only ever gone through it with a sense of curiosity and if he'd had to name it, awe.

"Same as always," he told her, staring unblinking at his device.

"Call, Joel. It's been two days and if you want to call, then I think she's been gone long enough to be worried."

Her hair had grown long enough to have some whips that moved when she twisted her head up from her game to meet his eyes with her own.

"I can't," he said. "She loved the church, and the church might not survive a police investigation."

"Because?"

He motioned to the open box on the desk, allowing his gaze to follow his head.

"That. And Lonnie, and all the murders. Who knows how long it will..."

He cut short there as the thought caught up to him, but his mind kept moving. The murders, so many murders, and Lonnie's feeling of betrayal. "Do you think..."

"What?"

"Lonnie. Do you think Lonnie might have killed my mother for revenge?"

"Lonnie's a teddy bear," Delilah said, smirking with a half-smile. "He'd never hurt your mother."

"A teddy bear? The serial-killer is a teddy bear?"

"Well," she said, batting her eyes once. "I *think* so. I'm pretty sure he wouldn't kill anyone he cares about. He and your mother have so much history." She paused and looked thoughtful for a moment. "No. No, he couldn't do that."

"Why not? He's killed before."

"And so have you," she said. The words caught his attention and seemed to pull his head around to her. It was true, and she had known it. And he knew she had known it. But she'd never *said it* outright before. "Would you ever kill me? It matters *who* is being killed, no?"

"I guess. But you weren't there for their fight."

"Call them," she said, sighing. "At least then you'll know."

"But what if she kept records, Delilah. What if she kept track of all the targets, and there's a list somewhere that I don't know about? What if the police find it? Then that's the end of our church."

"So what do you want to do?"

"There's nothing I *can* do. Can you do the sermons next weekend?"

She seemed to shrink away from him, but she smiled and nodded. "If you want me to, I will."

"It's what you wanted anyway, isn't it?"

Delilah shook her head.

"Not like this, no. I wanted a no-confidence vote, remember?" She shook her head at him as he stared on. "Not like this."

"We have to keep the church going, Delilah. She would want that."

———

Delilah remained with him throughout the rest of the week, staying dutifully on the couch, which kept him on edge. The minute he left his bedroom, her eyes were on him, and as soon as he did anything, she was right there by his side. He even had to inform her that he was going to the bathroom or she would follow him right down the hall. They'd fallen into stasis. He couldn't call the police and she stayed to provide 'emotional support'.

It was too easy to forget his mother. He'd been practiced at staying away from her so often that it was nothing to not see her for a day or two at a time. Delilah was a constant reminder that something had changed in his life, though he found himself just watching her back at times, wishing that the situation was different, and that she was there just for him, and he could hold her, kiss her, and touch her. But that would be a betrayal.

Instead, he watched her from afar as she lay on the couch, blanket rising and falling with each peaceful breath, drool seeping into the couch cushion beneath her head. The blanket had fallen from her, revealing her arm and shoulder through a t-shirt so thin that he could barely make out one of the larger freckles that rested on her collarbone. Her peace spread through him, as he knelt to gather the blanket from where it fell and lay it back over her. Just as he lifted it from the ground, he caught a splash of blue against the carpet. Holding the blanket in one hand, he bent further to see a blue splotch against the floor and something glinted next to it. With his index and thumb, he retrieved something from the floor, and his jaw dropped. He pulled his blanket-holding hand back to shift position so he could see it better, and the blanket fell back down on the carpet, pulling the rest of it off of Delilah's still-slumbering waist and short-clad hips, but he didn't bother retrieving it. Instead, he sat back, staring at the piece of glass, so flimsy that he thought he might break it just pressing it between his fingers. There was no mistaking the curve.

He stood and made his way across the room to his open kit. There, in the top, lay the syringe that he'd never used.

The blue liquid inside matched the spilled fluid on the floor, but the glass was the most damning since it held the same curve as the fleck between his fingers. He turned the syringe over in his hands to examine it more closely.

"Should I be worried?" His head shot up to see Delilah, still prone but both of her eyes trained on him.

"I'm not sure," he muttered, and placed the syringe back in the top of the kit. He kept his focus on her as he backed away from her, one foot after another. "What happened?"

Her eyebrows furrowed into a question mark.

"What do you mean?"

"I mean what happened to my mother?"

Her eyes shifted to his fingers, and then back to the syringe, and then popped open wide.

"Lonnie?"

His name made Joel begin to tremble and shake as he imagined his mother, standing here confronting Lonnie, perhaps reasoning with him, trying to get him to come back to her. He may have even gone along with it for a while — Lonnie could be convincing when he was in the right mood. Then, as soon as she let her guard down, perhaps trusting that he *had* decided to come over and join her again, the needle came out. Would she have fought, as defeated as she already was, when she saw what he did? Or, would she have done what Delilah now did, waited calmly for him to make up his mind about what to do next?

"Not just Lonnie," he decided as he spoke the words that he hadn't dared until that point to imagine. "Was it?"

He closed the kit, and latched it, leaving the syringe and instruments of death safely locked away from both of them. As he spoke, she spun sideways to a sitting position on the couch, legs tucked beneath her.

"I don't know what you're talking about."

His mind went back to the dream. *Why do you always deny me?* Her response drove into his gut like knives wedging between his ribs. The feeling was so palpable that he nearly collapsed. He felt her love, filling the space around him, receding back towards her as she clawed it back in the midst of his accusations. Emptiness crowded in.

"Joel, what are you talking about?"

"Lonnie. You were right the other day when you said he wouldn't kill her. There's one thing about him that's consistent. He does the Lord's work. It was Evie, until it was — is — you. You told him to get rid of her, didn't you?"

Her eyes darted from him to the killing box, then back again as she weighed her words. The last of her love sucked back into her body and, Lord or not, he could no longer feel her. But when the feeling left, something else took its place: a deep dream-like certainty that they were both alone. Alone in the church, alone in the room, and alone in the entire universe. He realized then that once again, what he'd thought was the Lord's love was another lie, a dangerous distraction from what was right in front of his face.

Of course Delilah had done it.

Even now the sense of bewilderment that she attempted to convey to him didn't reflect in her cautious eyes as they sought for an escape. She wasn't the Lord any more than Joel was — but poor Lonnie didn't know that. So when she'd said to jump, he had, and Joel's mother disappeared. Just like all the others, her body would never be found.

"It's a bit early to move in here, isn't it?"

"Joel, I think you're confused. Think this through. I'm here so you won't be alone while you search for her."

"Or you're here to make sure I don't look too hard, right?

Or that I don't look in the right place. When did he even clean up the mess? There had to be more than just the glass and the stain. Was that you? Or was it your job to distract me so that he could have time to do it?"

"Distract you. I did it all," he heard a voice, and for the first time noticed that Delilah's eyes had stopped shifting and instead focused heavily on the door behind him. Joel didn't have to turn to know who stood there, and the admission was like his heart being squashed beneath a falling volantrae. A tear ran down Delilah's right cheek.

"You weren't supposed to find out," she said, whispering the words out as she pulled the blanket up over her legs. "I love you, Joel. You and I are supposed to be the king and queen here. We're supposed to bring this church up together, the two of us."

She reached a thin arm for him, and he recoiled but didn't dare to back away. Somewhere behind him Lonnie stood.

"Joel, come talk to me. It had to happen. She was too powerful, and she'd never let the church evolve."

"It doesn't look to me like much has evolved at all." Then he felt the pinch on his neck and the room began to fade.

"Help me catch him, Lonnie. We don't want to hurt him."

Strong arms scooped beneath his shoulders, and he felt his legs pulled up beneath him and he felt himself lowered into the cushions. His eyes closed, but he could still hear the noises around him.

"He can hear us?"

"Yes, he can, Ms. Reynolds. Is there something you want to say before I send him to the Lord?"

"We're not sending him to the Lord, Lonnie."

"But he knows."

"Not everything is solved by sending people to the Lord. Sit over there."

He heard Lonnie shuffle away somewhere, and then Delilah began, her frail voice wavering through obvious pain.

"You weren't supposed to find out, Joel. It really was supposed to be you and me. But I guess you ruined that, so things will have to be different. Now, do you remember all of that stuff about Evie keeping records? I have those records. Thanks for letting me stay over — it was much easier to find them here. They were hidden in your mother's bedroom. She's got all of them, every single one, recorded on a data-coin, and now I have them — including the ones that you did.

"What's going to happen now is Lonnie is going to take you out of the church, and I'm moving in here. We'll make up some story, don't worry. And he's not going to kill you — not yet. You have a choice. If you come back here, then it better mean you're on board and coming to stand by my side. If you stay away, and don't *talk* about us to anyone, then that's your choice too. Not even to your father. Stay away, and I will miss you, but we don't have any reason to come find you. Right, Lonnie?"

"I suppose, Ms. Reynolds. Ms. Evie would have had him killed anyway."

"I'm *not* Evie. Things are going to be different. Joel gets to live. Do you have questions on that?"

"No, Ms. Reynolds."

"Good. Joel, you may be angry at me now. Some day, I hope you'll understand why I had to do what I did, and why all of this had to happen. The church does the Lord's work, and it must survive no matter what the cost."

No matter what the cost. How many times had his

mother told herself the same thing as she'd ordered death after death. No matter what the cost. Joel felt his consciousness beginning to fade as the sound of water and the blood in his veins overpowered the noises in the world around. Even Delilah's voice faded out of his mind.

CHAPTER 27

IT MIGHT HAVE BEEN hours or days before Joel awoke alone laying on the solitary bench with the heavy buzz of pedestrian traffic surrounding him. He pivoted himself around to the seating position, head swimming in the process until it finally stopped and he took in his surroundings. It seemed to be an old train station. Volantrae crowded the skyway above as most travelers passed by. Occasionally a straggler departed and swung down to the drop-off lane, leaving a passenger stranded below. Down here, the dredges of society lingered, Joel's new community.

He caught movement above as the news played on the single working holovid among the six such platforms he could see with a quick scan. This older model was only capable of showing a single image, no matter which direction one looked at it from. His breath left him as he saw the bright green and gold of the suit of Delilah's uniform across the stage. Beneath in bold three-dimensional letters: "New blood doubles membership in Austin Community Church".

"Sometimes we all have to make sacrifices for the Lord.

We can't always get that new car we want, or that new necklace. Sometimes we have to understand that the Lord doesn't only use *money* to get his message across."

The words were undeniably hers. The newscast transitioned from focusing on Delilah to the newscaster.

"The new face of Austin Community Church is bringing back some old questions. Against a slurry of accusations, the question still remains unanswered. Cult or church? Carol Barbary shares her experiences tonight on Channel 9 news."

He shook his groggy head and a pounding followed, shooting pain into his eyes. Whatever the blue stuff was, it had left him drained and throbbing... and extremely thirsty. He licked his dry lips, but the moisture evaporated as quickly as he layered it on.

"We may not like it. What the Lord wants and what we want may be different things," returned Delilah's voice, drawing his attention back as her voice seemed to crack. Joel didn't care about what the Lord wanted anymore. That guessing game had sucked too much of his life away already and had left him stranded in a train station. And without a mother.

Joel should have been decimated, but he could only feel a sense of freedom. His breath came light and fast, despite the pain that wouldn't recede from his brain. Emptiness pressed in on him, but it wasn't the same void desperate to be filled. He'd tried so hard to find the Lord's love that if he hadn't found it, then it wasn't there to be found. This longing was for Delilah, and her alone. His eyes wandered back to the holovid, but the news had already moved on. Conspicuously absent was any coverage of Evie.

The headache subsided enough for him to catch the eye of a family walking across the wide open area toward one of the gates. For a second he thought it was the Reynolds by the way they joked and prodded each other lovingly. The memory of dinner with them brought a smile to his lips until he recalled his mother fighting to keep him from going. Suddenly, it hurt to swallow. He blinked away the salt water in his eyes. The news switched back over to cover more of the Austin Community Church in the form of an interview with Delilah Reynolds.

"Don't get me wrong," came Delilah's voice. "The Lord will provide for those who do His work. And when He offers you something, you take it. But just because He helps sometimes, doesn't mean it's *all* the Lord's doing."

Joel stood to walk trying not to think about Delilah or Lonnie. As he shuffled forward, his foot collided with something soft. He bent to look and found a black bag that seemed almost bursting. He unzipped the top. Inside were clothes and when he reached down into the clothes, he felt something hard beneath them. His fingertips explored the object and he soon realized that Delilah must have packed his kill box. Doubtless if he looked around enough, there would be some cash-coins with enough money to get him a place and off to a good start. His fingers brushed against something papery and square. Joel pulled it out and flipped it into his hand to read handwriting he knew to be hers.

———

Joel,

Before you were in my life, I never understood what love meant. I knew that something was missing, but I couldn't be sure what it was. Now that you've been in my life, I know what that missing piece was. If there was some other life, I *could have everything I want — you, the church, and even your mother, as much trouble as she's created. I can never truly hate her for having brought you into the world.*

Millions of people now rely on me to bring them to salvation, so I hope that you understand I can't leave. That day when you asked me to run away with you was the hardest decision I've ever had to make. My heart screams yes. I can too easily imagine a simple life with you by my side bringing happiness. But as you probably know, the obligations we are born into often outweigh our heart's desires.

In this bag, you will find a token for transport to Portland, Oregon. That's the last place your mother had on file for where your father was. I don't know if he will want to see you or not, but I can only imagine that he will be proud of who you have become. I know I am, even if you disagree.

I love you, forever and always.

Delilah

P.S. Lonnie doesn't know about Portland.

————

With a throbbing temple, he picked up the bag and slung it over his right shoulder. Then he looked up at the digital billboards advertising departures and saw that the Portland train was already boarding. He could stay and look for his mother, though even as that thought materialized he already knew he would only find her if the police dismantled the church and dug up the grounds. He could make that happen, and spend the rest of his life in prison, having only succeeded in destroying what his mother had helped to create. Delilah had been right to assume that Joel wouldn't do that.

His mind went back to the hot days in the garden, so

many hours spent hand in hand, or in deep embrace — there was a love to it. If he hadn't been so myopically bound on his quest to find the Lord, a quest doomed to failure from the beginning, then perhaps things might have gone differently. He might have instead accepted Delilah's earlier advances, and he wouldn't have become the monster that she'd rationalized away.

He walked across the floor of the train station to the terminal where the train passengers loaded. Joel dropped the token into the counter machine and the arm lifted for him to pass. Then he stepped through, casting one more long glance over his shoulder just in time to catch Delilah on the stage again, looking every bit like Mary of Magdalen. But she wasn't. He knew that now. Casting his eyes downward watching his steps as he boarded onto the high-speed train, Joel chose a seat near the window. A minute later the train pulled out, and he watched the church pass with its giant cross plastered against the sky. The train continued to accelerate.

"Fourteen hours to Portland," came a computerized voice over the loudspeaker. Joel let out his breath and leaned his head back into the seat.

"Is anybody sitting there?" He jerked his head away from the window to see a blonde girl about his age standing in the aisle eyeing the seat beside him. Beyond her the train was sparsely occupied and empty seats abounded. He met her blue eyes and found recognition in them. "Do you remember me? Ella Shoemaker."

The Shoemakers had stopped attending the church several years before. Joel did remember, and he smiled the best he could.

"I remember."

"And you're Joel Emerson Haines?" The girl could barely contain the excitement in her voice. There was no point in denying it so he nodded and shrugged.

"You can sit here," he said, nodding to the empty seat beside him. "And it's just Joel. That's all."

"Joel," she repeated the words softly as Joel turned his attention back to the window. "What are you looking at?"

Her eyes followed his gaze as the cross grew smaller and smaller. "Oh, you're leaving."

"I'm leaving," he affirmed.

"Is it because your mother's not in charge anymore?"

The question dredged up recent events, but he tried not to react.

"No," he said with a thin smile. "I guess I'm leaving to find my own destiny."

"Me too. I've never been to Portland. Have you?"

Joel felt his shoulders relax as he turned to engage.

"I've never been out of Texas."

"Maybe we can find our destinies together," she told him, then her face flushed. "I mean just travel together for a while. It'll be nice to travel with someone I know."

Joel wondered how much anybody knows anyone else.

"At least as far as Portland," he told her, smiling as best he could. The cross disappeared from the window, replaced only by swampland as the train continued to pick up speed.

THE END

It takes a lot to put a novel out into the world. Not just the person sitting behind the keyboard. Oh, it is definitely an act of love to sit for hours bringing your worse fears and carving the most intimate parts of oneself onto vellum and then ruthlessly flinging the parchment into the wind, to be demolished, incinerated, spit upon...

But without the support of others, this story would never have seen the light of day. Specifically, I'd like to thank my wonderful wife, Hollee, who puts up with hours of me screaming at my keyboard or computer in frustration and, more commonly, only partially paying attention as I work through a plot twist in my mind. She somehow willingly entertains my obsession with clawing stories out of my brain and plopping them across my keyboard, and I love her all the more for it.

Also, my children, who are not yet old enough to read most of what I write, but will someday hopefully approve and understand that these pieces of myself that I put out into the world are there for them, too, so that if they find themselves similarly positioned—that is, taking guidance from a serial killer who channels the divinity—they have the wherewithal to question precisely what the truth of the situation might be.

I'm kidding, of course.

Not that there aren't serial killers in some churches, I just haven't come across one yet, personally.

I digress.

I'd also like to thank my childhood friends Ed and Jeremy for being my guiding stars. Most of this work is from my childhood, and I could say so much more. I can honestly profess that without these people who magically landed in my life, I would never have been the person who could adequately position these words.

And perhaps the most important of them all—you.

Thank you.

It is with humility that I say the most honor someone can find in this world is having said (or written) something good enough to be consumed by others. And if you are reading this, you've made it the entire way through.

Take a break. Give yourself a pat on the back and an auditorium full of applause. And now that that's done, right now, before you forget, go to Amazon (Book of Joel) or wherever books are sold and leave a review.

Or two.

Or three.

Heck, go crazy.

Again, and with all sincerity...Thank you.